LITTLE
krypton

by Bogart Endo

www.facebook "LITTLE krypton"

Cover Design by: Vince Pannullo Print by: RJ

communication

Printed in the United States of America

On cardboard box inked is "New York November 1990"

Shoot opens, panning Manhattan from atop the Empire State building. "Steppin'Out" spears its sharp keys, unifying different flashes of Metropolis to the sound of Joe Jackson's Punk classic

Bike Messengers with pink hair splicing through lanes, laugh as they defy rush hour traffic.

1 A truck passes by with a Giant HOLLYWOOD sign. Part of it (WOOD) cracks off to the pavement, while a pink haired messenger throws a fortune cookie at it
2 One of the messengers mysteriously appears by Keith Haring's crack baby mural "CRACK IS WACK" and nods approvingly riding by
3 Girls Vogueing (Madonna) in front of Astor Plaza barber shop, as they throw glitter at one of the Pink haired messengers, causing a rain of sparkles along 8th street. They laugh when he turns and strikes a pose
4 Cop car parked while three men come out in front of City Hall. One in pink cuffs, with a "Public Enemy" cap on, and a shirt that says "Fight the Power"
5 Yankee stadium shot from Pink scooter riding on the Tri-Boro, the lights of the electric monitor read, "The Sultan of Swat! George Herman Ruth"
6 Nuns waiting for a Bus in front of a Patrick Swayze poster "Ghost" genuflect, as a pink haired biker almost gets hit by the bus they're waiting on.

7 The last of the pink haired messengers jets by an Asian boy on thee Upper Eastside, who is apparently late for school, running along a silent block. Messenger brakes and stares at the boy entering the facility

QuincyX.Oxford is written above steel doors, as he jumps two wide steps and breezes thru a stoned entryway, where two guards sit behind a desk filled with graffiti and sunseeds await to greet him. Both guards are black, one fat lady, very dark, with thick glasses sitting next to a purple complexion darker one

Guard 1- Is the pizza shop opened up yet (trying to get a peak out the slow closing door)

There is a pizza shop (Sal's) across the street opposite the school

Nelson- no (slings backpack forward to dig for pen)
Guard 1- here, here, pencil (chin nodding toward the late sheet)

Nelson signs his name

Nelson Top'O'the'morning!

Runs up main flight of steps, then jumps around the stairs bend, over hearing Nadja (guard 2) speaking to her colleague

Guard 1- that kid sound like that ol'guy, in all them gangster flicks jah
Guard 2- Joyce, wuh'are you talk'n about
Guard 1- you know that ol'movie! "Here's look'n at you'kid" "Play it again Sam"
Guard 2- (Tone like she should know better) you know I don't watch none'a them brain wash'n movies Joy

Nadja puts video of a Spike Lee Joint in her bag "She's gotta have it"

Guard 2- (putting her bag away) Joyce you seen the Lotto numbers on the news Sunday…

Guard 1- I don't watch the news Jah, too depress'n

Nelson flies past the first floor, jumping out the second floor almost crashing into a preppie girl with a blue D on her sweater. He quickly sidesteps her and stomps down the hallway, unnoticing her glance to his red and white shirt. When he gets to his class (evenly mixed racially, most the taller boys being Black) he slows down, quietly entering

Ms. Kietz- Nelson you're going to fail my class (she speaks in lisps)

Ms Kietz watches Nelson make his way quietly to his chair next to a voluptuous blonde girl. The science teacher waits till he's seated then resumes her lesson

Darcy- hi sexy
Nelson- I saw that kid Patrick fight yesterdays
Darcy- yeah I know, I had to bail him out JAIL (checking her make up, in shell mirror)
Nelson-You bailed him out (slightly excited) whoa!
Darcy- yeah two thousand dollars
Nelson- Yowsers
Darcy- well he bailed me out once (snapping her shell mirror shut) costed three times that

Ms. Kietz overhears Darcy talking and sighs to the LIES coming out her mouth, while chalking the board. Her humourous grin is suddenly dowsed when a deep voice booms

Lamott- Yo! That Patrick's a bitch!!
Ms.Kietz- Lamott!
Darcy- (slamming her fist) shut the FUCK UP
Lamott- Whitey beat on a pudgy Mexican… TRY THAT ON A NIGGA
Ms. Kietz- Both of you don't stop right now! (Red in the face) to the deans office you go!!

4

Darcy and Lamott trade icey stares, then face forward

Ms. Kietz- Belzebub! (lets out huge breath then resumes lesson)
Darcy- (hushing) look how they act (staring at Lamott spitting on floor, gesturing wildly to Craig)

Nelson quiet not knowing what to say

Darcy- Don't be scared, if any of them fuck wit you, just tell me and I'll get the whole Sicillian mafia here, my uncles a MADE MAN, Martin Scorcese did a movie about him

A Hispanic girl in the back is trying to get Nelson's attention, until she see's Lamott staring at her, to which she quickly stops

Nelson- when I called you yesterday why was the phone so buzzy
Darcy- oh (pausing to think) oh yea, I was taking shower
Nelson- wish you could'a tol me, I jerk off to that (mimes fist up and down)
Darcy- Ooh, you're bad (smiling) you can call me when... (Scream belts out, cutting her words)
Craig-CHOY-YOY-YOING'CHING'CHANG-PYUNG-YANG-YING-FING-PEKING
Ms. Kietz- That's it! Craig, to the Deans office! NOW! (Ms. Kietz watches Taheem, Lamott, and Hendrix give Craig the thumbs up walking out)
Craig-Don't forget my eggroll mister PAY-SEE-MAY-MAY (leaving with his eyes squinted)

Same Hispanic girl that tried to get Nelson's attention, speaks to her friend quietly near the window

Ana- was that Nelson he was talking too?
Tanya- yea, I think he was

Ana- I don't like that girl (giving dark focus to Darcy) when he was sitting with us (Latina's) they (The Blacks) didn't care. Fucking'blanquita getting him in MIERDA
Tanya- shhhh… that girls a hoody, she might hear
Ana- I don't care!

Nelson turns hearing Ana's voice. She can't see him, all her attention is on Darcy. Taheem stares at Nelson menacingly

Darcy- Don't worry, Patrick's coming to pick me up today, you can leave with us
Nelson- (looking down) ok

~Scene End

Int- Homeroom bell rings, Ana is in her chair with an eye on the door watching students fly in. Suddenly Nelson enters just missing Taheem's group putting their coats in the closet

She calls out to him

Ana-HAY!
Nelson- (sarcasm) why ya'whisper'n
Ana- Why you hang around that girl?
Nelson-who's'ya talk'n bout
Ana- you know (Nodding toward Darcy just walking in)
Nelson- I don't know
Ana- she LIES and sticks her WIDE ASS out like a donkey, tryin to cause a riot to the BLACKS
Nelson- (Ignores tantrum) wheres'ya'wanna'eat lata
Ana-WOULD YOU FIGHT OVER THAT ASS
Nelson- you know they say, if you have to fight, you already lost
Ana-huh?
Nelson- (Ignores tantrum) NEW SUBJECT!! where we eating
Ana- (stares for awhile) I don't know, what you gett'n

Nelson- I got a dolla so I'm gett'n a bagel

Ana- I'm gett'n a sandwich at Sal's, you can have half
Nelson- oh…alright, thanks

Ms. Pembell walks in. The homeroom and math teacher

Ms.Pembell-Everyone, sit (she opens her attendance book and starts going down the list of names)

Nelson goes to kiss Ana before she sits but she pulls away right at the last

Ana- MAN did you brush (unwrapping piece of gum) here you cochino
Nelson- thanks (he gets it quick in the mouth and feels the cold of her nails poke his lips, which leaves some specks of sparkle as Ms. Pembell calls his name) Here!
Ana- (Ana's full name is called) Here! (Swiping Nelson's lips with the wrist part of her sleeve)
Nelson- (muffling) it's gone!

From front of the room Taheem watches

Lamott- Yo that gook look like Jackie Chang
Taheem- (although Hendrix and Lamott laugh, Taheem stays straight faced) that nigga Craig still ain't back yet
Hendrix- I bet they called his Medusa (fingers twisting his dread locks)
Lamott- If he get in trouble, I'm'a slap that kid right there (looking at Nelson)
Taheem- Hold up (Craig comes through the door looking upset)

Ms.Pembell checks his name present on the attendance and stays quiet

Craig- (kicking chair down) YO, I gotta stay after school for like thirtyMINUTES! I caught Levi in a fucked up attitude!

Lamott see's Nelson take off his mustard
colored J crew jacket and keeps staring

Lamott- you wanna take that jacket
Hendrix-(Strong Jamaican tone, swinging red, black and
yellow belt) who gon' wer dat-shit it Yung-tight
Craig- I'm'a give it to my lil'cousin
Hendrix- (in a very nasal tone, sitting on top his desk, foot on
chair) Mon, he not gone worry'tear
Taheem- Chill this school shit's jus started (staring at
Nelson) little too early for jack'n coats too little

Period Bell rings and students flock out both back
and front doors

Darcy stares darkly at Ana leaving with Nelson

Ana- Wait for me in front, I'm be taking yearbook shots with
Tanya
Nelson-k

_Scene end

Int- Nelson stands inside a burgundy doorway, five doors in
all, which is the entrance of the school, holding for Ana. Two
minutes into it, a kid his height with the same facial features as
Hendrix, then another twin with identical hair texture as Hendrix
stand right next to him. They stare slightly, then both mind their
business. Nelson moves to the side to avoid any static, suddenly
Hendrix and Craig pop out

Hendrix- Chew go on now rude boy, you know'a'jah duty
Dante- STAY quiet blud'clut

8

Hendrix- ay'yo Ferno, tell this batte'bwa to take him down'tair and wash'dem'Ta-Bull

Ferno- Jwa no if you don't, Medusa not gon'key you no break, when Levi'dem call up d'howse

Dante-Blud'clut! Jwa'don't gimme'no break right now! (Dante spit's gum into his fist, then beams it at a parked car, walking down second ave towards the back exit of the school, where the Dean Levi's office is) ay'yo dirty! (Hollers at Ferno, going toward Sal's pizza) save half me slice for homeroom!

Ferno- Eat goat!

Dante-WHAT

Ferno-GOAT NUTT INSIDE JA'AZZ'HOLE

    Suddenly Nelson loses sight to a pair of cold fingers covering his eyes

Ana- shhhhh, who is it cochino

Nelson- Dee, whys'you come this way (pulls her hands off)

Ana- I hit Bobo up for some money

Nelson- wher'rizzy

Ana-He's eating lunch with Abner downstairs

Nelson- he eats school lunch? (looking at his lunch tickets, which are dated and numbered)

Ana- yea and?

Nelson- and I thought these was just good for toss'n (flicks one off his index finger, frisbeeing the ticket onto a black girls weave across the street)

Ana- you're such a troublemaker I swear

Nelson- ready to go

Ana- not yet, you seen Tanya?

Nelson- no, why

Ana- I was suppose to, (looks up the block) what time is it

Nelson-twelve fifteen

Ana- let's go

Nelson- want to give her few more…

Ana- nah it's alright, she said if she wasn't here by ten after to jus go

Nelson notices the Crew brothers (Hendrix,Ferno) giving Darcy a dirty look as she walks into school with high puffed up hair carrying a brown paper bag

She acts as if they're invisible, walking by with her head held high

Craig- (whispering) stank'hoe

Darcy keeps her mouth shut and walks through door

Hendrix- Dat a good way to win the girl affection (smirking)
Craig- Fuck that WHITE bitch, BEND HER BIG ASS OVER

Leaves fall in slow motion, from trees surrounding the school. When the final leaf hits the pavement, Craig kicks a domino strangely on the ground with his boot, the domino pops up and hits a funeral car. The Car alarm sounds

Nelson inside a tenement away from school, with no doorman, just bells and mailboxes, where Ana is sharing a ham'n cheese with him. A faint sound of a car alarm is heard.

Ana- you heard that?
Nelson- (puts half a sandwich on the step and glares at Ana) huh?
Ana- spooky noise (goes back to eating but notices Nelson still eyeballing her) why you'starin
Nelson- you know your lips look like rubber everytime you take a bite
Ana- they do not you ungrateful child
Nelson-what I should be happy somebody's feed'n'me
Ana- exactly cochino

A resident of the building steps thru and slams the door

Resident lady- look I know it's getting cold out there and you need a place to eat (opening second door inside) but just make

sure you don't leave anything behind
Ana- sorry, we'll make sure there's no mess
Resident lady- good, cause if you don't the RATS will! (Slams a second door*BOOM!)

Quiet sets in

Nelson- I's can getcha' free tickets to the show
Ana-what show? YOUR SHOW!
Nelson- I can get three in, but only on Weds'day
Ana- what time, my mom wants to see it too
Nelson-nine
Ana- it's a Japanese play?
Nelson- nah, but there's Japanese people in it cuz' of the war back then, I mean actors
Ana-oh...
Nelson- I only come in few times. I make friends with this army dude and he gives me food, not food but like chocolate
Ana- oh
Nelson- yea but at the end... (Ana cuts in)
Ana- Don't tell me the end! I'm gonna see it right
Nelson- Sure, if you want
Ana- then don't kill it for me (brushing off her black shirt, snatching a soda can out of Nelson's hand, taking a sip) we better get back

Nelson stuffs the rest of the Hogie in his mouth and opens the door

Ana- Hold up (she crumples up the paper it came in, rolling it into a ball) now let's go
Nelson- (Jerks the crumpled sandwich wrapper out her hand and tosses it on steps) thought us rats were supposed to litter
Ana- (shakes her head) loco
Nelson- whats that mean
Ana- crazy

~EndScene

Int- Ms.Owens art class, the students are doing group projects with students of class 9-221

Kathy- Angel why you put so much paint in this water, its all ink (Pointing at the plastic cup)
Luis- Jesus mami! Jus get another cup, shit!
Kathy- you get it!
Luis- (speaks to Nelson) you believe these stupid puta's

Luis goes to get a cup muttering incoherently when Kathy says

Kathy- that girl is staring at you
Nelson- who?

Nelson looks over and sees Darcy staring right at him

Kathy- you gonna go ova there or what
Nelson- I knows' that girl
Kathy- I hope she ain't trying to stare at me (spoke wit attitude)

Nelson gets up and starts walking. At the same time Ana see's Nelson walking over to Darcy and tries to cut him off. In her haste, she accidentally bumps into Taheem

Ana- sorry
Taheem- why don't you watch where I'm goin' Bitch
Ana- Excuse me! (Puts on brakes)
Taheem- Yo, keep stepp'n
Ana- don't call me bitch ok
Taheem- (sarcastically in a bratty voice) oh-kay-ee
Ana- CAN I GET THRU (noticing Taheem's chair blocking her way between tables)

Taheem moves his chair in to let her squeeze by then grabs her painting, tearing it, witnessing it sway to the floor

Ana- Fucking asshole!
Taheem- (still repeating Ana) Fucking asshole

Out the blue Nelson picks the two pieces up from the floor and starts walking to Ana. Taheem grabs him from the back with a choke

Ana- let him go!
Taheem-let him go-oh-oh

Nelson tries to stay calm but is losing air, after a long second, Taheem let's go

Taheem is then hit with two blows right to the chest. Ana, shocked

Taheem- ouch? (smiling, unfazed)

Nelson waits to be hit back, strangely standing without his hands up
The only move Taheem makes is back to his seat. Nelson looking calm outward, but stammering in his heart, manages to get few words out

Nelson- Ana, you wants'me to save this for'ya (holding up her two pieces of torn art)
Ana- (surprised a full blown fight didn't come out the situation, she quickly moves) come on! (Grabbing him by the Wrist and pulling toward a table far off, as Ms.Owen steps in from the hallway
Ms. Owen- Nelson what are you doing here with nine, one, oh, nine, (9-109) you're supposed to be back there with nine, two, two, one (9-221)
Ana- I'm showing him how to mix colors, blend
Ms. Owen- Show him another time!

Ana- But… (Nelson kisses her cheek, gets up, moves away)
Nelson- (Ana's eyes paste on him) I'll be ok

   The walk seems longer then usual across tables. When he gets back to his group, he feels Angel climbing his back

Angel- (almost whispering) yo loco, you know that
Nelson-what?
Luis- that kid lives' round my way, trust me he probably thinks you too small to punch, cuz I seen him fuck my older brother up, and he in highschool
Nelson- well it makes me happy not to be in your family
Luis- iight then (he turns back to angel) I tried to tell him papi

   Darcy comes over to Nelson, while Ms.Owen is helping a group near the front, she did not see the melee that just occurred

Darcy- (talking fast) I'm goin to the bathroom, after I leave ask Ms.Owen for the boys room pass, I'll wait for you
Nelson-k

Darcy walks over to Ms. Owen waiting to go out, she leaves in a flash. Nelson follows right after

   Zooming close up near the windows can be seen Ana's profile, steaming from watching Darcy ask Nelson out

   ~EndScene

   Int- Nelson and Darcy in a stall in the girl's bathroom

Darcy- Its bad right
Nelson- you're bleeding
Darcy- have my period

Nelson- oh

Darcy- that's why I pushed your hand away, I don't want your fingers to get smelly

Nelson- I don't care (pushes hand down again)

Darcy- (chuckles) sexy, you're too cute (touches again) stop!

Nelson-(motionless, angry) whats'wrong!

Darcy- nothing, it's just I don't want to do it like this when I'm...dirty

Nelson- It's so hard tho' (looking at his crouch, gripping her fingers) why we even start this then

Darcy- I thought it stopped (holds Nelson by the face) call me tomorrow early, I'll check if I'm still flowing.

Nelson- (disappointed) whateva

Darcy- don't be like that (pinches his cheek) and if I am, check me again Sunday

Shaking his chin softly

Darcy- ok tough guy (trying to break the ice look on Nelson's face) k'boo

Nelson- (reluctantly) alright

Darcy- (smiling, tongue kissing Nelson passionately) we better get back (rebuttoning her jeans, and tightening her belt)

Nelson- (slight smile) yea

Darcy- Wait! (she wipes Nelsons mouth of lipstick) k, let's go

   A speck of sparkle gloss from Ana's nail polish falls from Nelson's lips and floats to the floor, the speck is followed by the camera, which lands on his shoe, the shimmer is viewed closely and then pans out again with Nelson sitting, staring out of Mr.Sapt's history class, with Homeroom bell ringing a second and last time

Mr. Sapt- Remember, the test is going to be on primitive society and Mesopotamia, the first civilization

   Children rush out except for two sitting way back

Hermin- (packing up slowly) those goons didn't show up for the whole class

Nelson-Who

Hermin-Taheem and them

Nelson-why care?

Hermin- I heard about your sixth period "Art of Fighting" exhibition

Nelson-what?

Hermin- It's no secret, you hit Taheem

Nelson- only in the chest (speaking as if he should know how small he is to Taheem)

Hermin- Dude! That's still a bold act!

Nelson- forget it Erm, if he wants too, he could probably fuck me up anytime

Hermin- that's not the point. You stood up to him, (deepens his voice) where I'm from people bully people all the time and they can't do a thing'bout it. That was a good thing you did

Nelson-where in Queens?

Hermin- Jugoslavija (a voice tears between them)

Mr. Sapt- though I love for you to carry on fine gentlemen. (Grinning) you will have to do so somewhere other then here

Nelson- lata Erm

Hermin- (text and notebook along with bookbag stacked in one arm giving Nelson a pound with the other) peace

Hermin leaves first, Nelson rushes out next with the teacher slamming door behind. A second later Nelson can be seen squeezing through a maze of kids, all the way to Homeroom. When he gets near the doorway a girl dashes toward him

Ana- (grips his wrist) HURRY nobody saw you

Nelson-huh?

Ana- Lamott, Hendrix, Taheem and all them, they didn't show

Nelson- I has'tah go to homeroom anyway, I need my jacket

Ana- Already picked it up for you (opens her bag to let him see)

Nelson- (calmly) Ana (grinning at her) we gonna do this everyday

16

Ana- (sarcastically) maybe

Nelson- (brushing past swiftly) Move!

Ana- (tredding beside him) alright just wait, if they don't see you till after the weekend they prolly forget bout it

Nelson- look if we run now, they're gonna fuck wit me whenever they want, trus'me Ana, I have to be straight'up

Ana watches Nelson walk into homeroom Craig, Taheem, and Lamott are not present

After five long minutes the exit bell rings to which students empty out

Nelson- Maybe they scared (playing)

Ana- not funny

Nelson- come on (pulling her sweater) lets go

As they walk down the main floor, toward exit, three cops and a flush red faced boy walk into the school office. Boy has a T-shirt, no jacket and one of his jean pockets is inside out

Cop 1- Call this kids parents

Mr.Rosebaum-What happened?

Cop3- boy got robbed and roughed up

Mr. Rosebaum- young man what's your name?

Mario- Mario (licking puffy lip)

Mr. Rosebaum- (hand on shoulder, gliding him to a phone on receptionist's desk) do you know the thugs who did this to you son?

Mario- nah (looking down)

Cop1- (walkie-talkie going off) Comitsky hea'!WHAT

Walkie talkie- (beany voice) "We got a four eight-eight on 96th and York, seems like assistance is needed"

Cop1-five minutes copy (hand radio "COPY")

Cop2- Mr. principal you got this under control?

Mr.Rosebaum- yes gentlemen (shaking hands, showing policemen out) thank you
Cop2- (taking a watch out his pocket) I found this on the floor (nudging Mario with it) yours?
Mario-YES!
Cop2- (grinning) you'll be fine (pats the boy on back then leaves)

Nelson, Ana and few other kids are standing by the office door, front and back

Ana- (thru muttering students) you see that, I bet that's why they wasn't in homeroom today
Nelson- hows'ya know it was them
Ana- (with a comical stare) who else beats up and robs people (sarcastically) an'da'lay co'chino
Nelson- you seem to like to call me chinese, I don't mind
Ana-cochino don't mean Chinese, COCHINO means pig
Nelson-What?
Ana- (smirking) nothing, lets walk

_EndScene

Int- Ana and Nelson on corner of 55th and 8th, passing Blimpies, a sandwich shop Nelson's building sits above

Nelson- Want the tickets tonite
Ana- aren't you performing tonight
Nelson- yea, after the show I'm'a get tickets
Ana- if I'm not awake give them to my brother
Nelson- iight (rushes away)
Ana- (catches Nelson before he can escape) bye papi (pulls him kissing his cheek)
Nelson-bye
As Nelson walks in his building the doorman opens up for him and gives an approving stare

Joel- how many times I gotta tell you Bruce LEE-VAH Our women ALONE! (smiling)

Nelson- SO, you're married to Phillipino chick, it's only fair I tap your well as well

Joel- leave the Latina's alone or else (Tony Montana voice) chu'gonna cee the south Bronx Come out of me papi

Nelson- dude you're not from the South Bronx, you from East Tremont

Joel- (tip of cracking up) OOH! You think you smart delivery boy!! If you so wise Mr. Wong, how is it you don't know us Latino's are taking over the world

Nelson-yea'BeanWorld

Joel- talk like that's gonna make me bring my son down, to give you the business

Nelson- I'm shaking in ME BOOTS (Joe grabs and puts a "Blimpies" gift card in his pocket)

Joel- I see you working that hot lil'Puerto Riquena right there, now you can buy her a hot chocolate Holme'slice

Nelson- man that girl gots'mah balls in her pocket

Joel- yea, you should tell that to my wife, she used to have mine in her heart, but now I think she just ate them like huevos

Before they can joke anymore, a bum crusty black woman, smelling putrid walks out the lobby

Nelson has a look of shame

Joel- you're papi'chulo be buggin

Nelson-uh, yea (uncomfortably)

Joel- (weak attempt at humor) you should tell him to save you a piece, say daddy "What you gonna poke that all by yourself"

Nelson- (embarrassed) stepfather

~EndScene

19

@ }—'--,----------------2

6DEGREES

Int- Stepping out the elevator to an abysmal blue hallway, very long and fully carpeted, Nelson walks to his apartment and opens an unlocked door

Oddly a piano sits in the middle of the living room, behind it a queen sized bed, where within lay his naked stepfather, He is covered in scaly patches of pink blots across his body, and dead skin flakes, scrap the floor around him

A floor model T.V. with a cable dialer is next to the piano, and where Nelson stands by the door is a walk in closet

Nelson goes to his room, which is past the kitchen thru a   hallway that ends at the bathroom turning right

His room is the same size as the living room, with three huge windows showing a diamond view of eighth avenue. There's a desk, junior bed near the glass and two closets

After standing for a moment, Nelson walks over to a phone and calls someone

Nelson- hi Sheila can I speak to…oh… practice, I didn't know… sorry Sheila, I'll call lata (hangs up then clicks on radio)

Radio- (Three beat intro) Your club and concert calendar!! Tonight at Roseland performing their smash hit "I don't know anybody else" from the "Dreamland" album, RCA House sensation Black Box! And at club Mars where "Frankie Knuckles" spins the wheel's of steel, over four floors of Acid-House and Dj R-son setting the ceiling a'blaze in his famed Hip Hop Suite! With special guests Brand Nubian. Last but not least, don't forget the open roof triple X Reggae lounge down Tribeca, where "Lion Hart Ben" will be mixing the world best Jamaican Rum Mix!

Nelson walks away from the radio takes off his coat and stretches his legs and arms, then walks to the door closing it tight, before pumping it up

Radio-…And performing the number one club HIT "The Power" SNAP!! Will be performing live at Sound factory, located on twenty seventh and…

Nelson closes his eyes and a moment later music begins to play, he warms up, but a phone rings before he can move

Nelson- YES… yea I called like minute ago… you don't need tickets, you and Alec is comin wit' me…AT SIX… knock loud… hold up, ask Al if he beat Zelda… funny… you're the one who plays the generic Sega Genesis…TECMO BOWL'HOMO! WHO? (hangs up)

Nelson looks out the window with radio fading out.

Fading in place of the dance music is a melancholy violin solo. Itzhak Perlman's rendition of Ennio Morricone's love theme *cinema paradiso* expressing Nelson's mysterious gaze out his giant window

Camera zooms down to street and creates a black circle around a man hand trucking a grandfather clock. The circle shrinks to the digit twelve on the clock, stopping there for a moment before totally closing up, leaving the scene in total darkness, til voices can be heard

Int- Alec and Seph are in the staircase of the fourth floor, where Seph's apt is right next door to

Alec- Them nigga's in five, oh, one, (501) is no joke
Seph- man that whole crew is pussy except for Hardaway, he iight

Alec- Gilky koo'for whiteboy
Seph- man all them white kids is wanna'be's down there, look how phony they be act'n
Alec- (raising a shoulder) that's the life of a city kid'yo
Seph- (annoyed) Life of city kid, them kids chose that shit, they folks got money, they don't gotta BE PIRATES
Alec- maybe (see's a slim Jim jerky wrapper on the floor) Yo what time's the play
Seph- What'play?
Alec- that show in the Game Museum, wit Nelson butt naked
Seph- whoa, I was supposed to wake that nigga up for that play (walking out the staircase, Al following) hurry FAGGOT!

_Scene fades

{Note}

1 The father whom is written as "Pop" is the stepfather of the protagonist. He is a manic depressive suffering from psoriasis and a bitter man, sleeping mostly and drinking the other. Attributes of "Pop" are not looked in on in the story, but from the little bit of dialogue between the two you can tell he is epic fail. The real father is never discussed, only that he is of Japanese heritage and dead from suicide, PTS attributed from the Vietnam War. The mother, who re-married shortly after, abandons her new husband and son, which is the reason for the son's lone parent.

2 The MONY clock referred to in this chapter is from the Hell's Kitchen area of New York. Before the Westside skyscraper boom of the late 90's, a lighted tower telling time and temperature stood atop a roof of a corporate building on the corner of 56th and Broadway. The residents of the neighborhood would look up when the area skyline was lower.

3 Game Museum which is referred to in this chapter is really the ATA off-Broadway theatre. It was founded in 1976 by James Jennings and has held actors Danny Aiello, Dennis Quaid, Bruce Willis, Kevin Spacey, Edie Falco along with many other's that graced it's stage. The building in itself is a landmark (pre-World War I building) and is badly in need of an upgrade.

4 "Football Head" Alec from my best memory always had a narrow face and spear long head. The term "Football Head" was a nick name for many years but always playful.

Int- Nelson deeply sleeping gets awakened by his stepdad, standing naked in his doorway

Pop- NELSON SHIT SON OF BITCH, WHY BLACK LIKE SHIT COLOR PEOPLE WAKE UP ME!!
Nelson-what?
Pop-YOUR FRIEND PUNCH DOOR
Nelson- oh (Nelson realizes its pitch in his room and looks up at the MONY clock for time) DAMN, I'm late!
Pop- LATE... (cackles) FOR WHAT, YOU HAVE JOB?
Nelson- no I'm doing a show
Pop- (laughing) WASTING TIME ON SHOW, BUT SCHOOL NO GOOD, NEVER CLEAN HOUSE, NEVER LOOK NORMAL IN AMERICA, DO BAD ON TEST, ALWAYS LYING TO ME!! WHAT YOU DO MAN?? YOU WANT TO BE BUM LIKE NIGGER FRIEND!!HAHAHAHAHA!!!
Nelson- yeah, better then Korean
Pop- (going back to living room) MR. SHIN SAID HE GIVE YOU FOOD BUT ONLY NITE TIME, DADDY HAVE NO MONEY OK
Nelson- ok
Pop- fucking last place shit son of bitch

His Korean stepdad leaves the room and Nelson runs out the apt looking like a disaster

Seph- (talking fast, poking him with his fingers) wake up, wake up, wake up
Nelson- (punching aggravated) FUCKING'FUCKING!
Alec- Nelson the show starts now (eyebrows raised)
Nelson- (frustrated) Seph! Why didn't you get me at five when you called?
Seph- I didn't know what time your show started!
Nelson- (walking back in to get dressed) Alec you brought Zelda? (Classic Nintendo)

Alec- nah, but I finally beat that game
Nelson-Seph!
Seph- What! You asked me if he beat it
Nelson-(Slams door)

~Scene fades

Int- Nelson gets out the elevator in the Lobby, Al and seph are sitting on the sofa

Alec- (walking over to him) Show me that new step you learned at Emerald City
Nelson- hold up I gotta drop this (He drops a letter in the mailbox where the elevator buttons are)
Alec-what's that? (Referring to letter)
Nelson-Les Guardant sent a form (Al looks curious) it's nutt'n, what'd you want to see?
Alec-that new step I saw you do last week at Emerald City. (Positive energy) SMOOTH CRIMINAL!
Nelson-oh you mean (Nelson starts doing a version of it)
Alec-(going bezonkers) YO' IS THAT A MOONWALK

Nelson starts doing the step in full

Alec- how'd you learn that (tenants of the building walking in see Nelson dancing and google)
Nelson- I don't know, I jus did (wondering why it's a big deal, as tenants stare)
Alex-YOU GOTTA TEACH ME THAT
Seph- I jus saw that Jim guy. And he looked pissed
Nelson-Where?
Seph- In Blimpies
Nelson- we better go (Nelson speed walks out the lobby peering up to see the Mony clock) yikez! Hope my part didn't come up (Seph and Alec speed walk with him)

Scene fades with Nelson's back viewed along with his head shakily trodding to the Game Museum, looking up watching the flags over theater sway to a six'clock sky

*BLACKOUT

A gunshot can be heard

Then a roar of clapping storms in from outside double green doors, which Jim opens a second later letting audience patrons out

Jim- Elevators are to the right or you can walk down its only three flights. Thank you for coming! And hope you all, a wonderful, safe evening

A lady glamorously dressed is speaking to Alec

Lady in White- so give him this card, and tell him to call me (raising a brow) you do know him, you're not pulling my chain
Alec- YEA'We live like two blocks from each other
Lady in White- (smiling) ok I believe you. Tell him to call right away I need to fill a spot in the worst way kid ←
Alec- he'll call you, I'll make sure
Lady in White- Thanks cutie (pinches his cheek)

Nelson comes out another door on the side, face still powdered. Seph and Alec run over to him with big cheesy smiles, not seeing the stagehand holding lights from the show step in Nelson's path

Some of the stage lights drop

Stagehand- that's (stops calmly and looks all around) gonna cost a few pennies
Jim- (Yelling) Nelson! Get back in, change and go home (Nelson walks back head down) NOW WHO'S GONNA PAY FOR THESE?!
                                                                    ~SceneEnd

26

Int- Seph and Alec are wiping glass off their jeans outside the theatre when Nelson pops out, pocketing a rag he had to wear for the show off his forehead

Seph- what'happened?
Nelson-nuttin
Alec- you're still in?
Nelson- Who else is gonna go naked! Plus they only have two shows left
Seph- yea, and that is a WEDGE and half up the AZZ'CRACK bro

Nelson gives Seph the finger

Alec- (laughing) when Jim was yelling at you, you looked like one of them Asian slaves in China making sneakers
Nelson- we make football heads too
Seph- (Cracking up cause the whole neighborhood calls Alec football head) CONE HEAD!!!
Alec- Na, for real, those Asian places get paid like ten cents an hour to make fake Rolex's
Nelson- That's why'ya head got a "Made in Thailand" stamped on it?
Seph- (cracking up) AHHHHHH!!
Alec- shut UP MONKEE!!
Seph-Egghead
Nelson- (breaks it up) let's go, Pizza-pizza!

_Scene Fades

Int- Luigi's Pizza: Nelson, Seph and Alec are sitting down with pepperoni slices and few cans of soda

As they eat, an acquaintance from the neighborhood enters the Pizzeria

Seph- Yo here come Rakim (steps in rocking Beastie Boy shirt)
Rakim- Damn this little nigga Nelson eatin like an Ethiopian
Alec- Na man he jus performed, we comin out this show he done
Rakim- WORD! (Smiling, big white teeth) Coo-cool (giving Nelson a pound) so should I get a pen for this nigga
Nelson- QUIT IT, it's off Broadway
Rakim- Broadway! Shit let me find out you on Broadway, have the whole Fam' up in there
Seph- how you all the way up hea?
Rakim- my cousin Craig from Harlem down here see'n a movie
Nelson- this cousin of yours, he wouldn't happen to go to ... (Rakim cuts him off)
Rakim- yea, he go to your school, I'm come'n in wit'him on Monday
Nelson- Craig's your cousin! (Alec and Seph are clueless)
Rakim- yea (confused) why?
Nelson- Hold up, you and Craig on Monday, to Oxford?
Rakim- yea I was up in Jew'Vee for some joy'riding bullshit in Mount Vernon, jus got out like few days ago
Nelson- so you go to Oxford?
Rakim- YES man!! Grill'n me like Barney fuck'n MILLER
Seph- Nelson look like that Chinese narc on "TwentyOne Jump Street"

They all start laughing

Nelson- I punched one of his buddies

They all stop laughing

Rakim-What?
Nelson- It not what you think
Rakim- (tense) well goes on nigga
Nelson- it's a long story but trus'me I ain't a threat, the kid I punched, rode it out
Rakim- sound like a pussy

28

Nelson- nah, he's no pussy I can tells'ya'that

Rakim- how come he didn't fuck you up?
Nelson- It's not like he couldn't (pause) I don't know
Rakim- Look y'all he come'n'right now, I'ma' grab'm before he get hea
Nelson- wher'rizzy?
Rakim- he went to get a sandwich (pointing to Blimpie's through Luigi's gigantic glass walls) lata y'all (leaving) see you Monday (to Nelson)
Alec- you got beef
Nelson- I don't think so
Seph- what you mean you don't think so… you PUNCHED, I'd say that's beef
Nelson- well static gotta go both ways right… I mean both sides are goin, CORRECT
Alec- so what you say'n
Nelson- I'm saying I don't have anyone to back me up. You guys don't go there, everybody there is from Uptown
Seph- so if something happen's your just gonna let them do whateva?
Nelson- I'll fight if I has'tuh, but worse comes to worse I'm gonna transfer
Alec- one O four (104) is like that, mad headz be roll'n in cliques
Seph- (nutty) WHAT!! Nobody be doin nuttin' up there!! (quickly turning to Nelson) you know what they be doin (body gesturing like a stereotypical black teen) except it's a bunch'a fake ass white kid's
Nelson- Ok (not seeing the point)
Alec- I don't know… them five O one boys... (Cut off)
Seph- Five O one nutt'n, Nelson's more live then all them Stuyvesant town bitches!! (rambling on) that ain't even no real projects
Nelson- could'a fooled me, that's a lot of red buildings
Alec- waiting list dude, they even got their own security
Nelson- that's where that gang comes from (looking at Alec)
Seph-THANK YOU!

Alec- not all them kids rize from there, a few them be from L.E.S

Seph- L.E.S kids is bitches too

Alec- nah dude, some them'kids can fight, like Gilky

Nelson- who's Gilly?

Seph- This big mouth nigga

Nelson-(giggling) ok

Seph- White kid who look like he does heroin through the lips (Seph puts his elbows inside out like Mick Jager and starts girating, sucking his cheeks in at the same time) he walk around like this all day (Seph sticks his tongue out far as he can, bobbing like a retard) like Steven Tyler his daddy

Nelson- (cracking up) Heroin through what

Alec- I bet he earns your respect by the end of school year (suddenly a loud holler cries from the back)

Danny- Hey!! We gonna'clos'a the store now, you FINISH

Nelson- yea! Sorry

Danny- No sorry! Just'a keep it down, if you want to give five minutes no problem, just'no yelling

Seph- I'm trying to teach this kid something (pointing at Alec) sometimes he can't hear too good

Danny- you sound'a like my wife, sometime she try to teach me something, I say'ah FUCK IT!! JUS SUCK'A MY DICK!!

Nelson laughs out loud

Alec- yo that dude said suck his dick

Nelson- COX!! (Nelson licks two of his fingers and slaps Seph in the forehead)

Alec-(laughing hard) Nelson!! Tell my wife here (bumping his nose across the table) to just shut the fuck up, and suck myDICK!

Nelson-COX!! Say'n (crybaby voice mimicking Seph's word to Danny) sorry sir, I'll keep it down promise I will, but my friend needs to learn... (cutting his words, doing pizza guys voice) AH JUST SUCK'A MY DICK!!!

Alec- (going over to cox Seph but suddenly knocks his can of soda all over himself) FUCK!!

Nelson stares at Alec going ape shit

Seph- COX! (slapping Alec hard on the head but Alec grabs his finger and tries to twist it)
Nelson-COX!! (slaps hard)
Alec- CHILL MAN! THIS MY NEW FRESHLY SQUEEZED!! (Trying to soak up his jeans with paper napkins)
Seph-AH, JUST'SUCK'A MAH'DICK!!

They crack up so loud that Danny comes out the saloon style doorway of the kitchen with a wooden spatchler

Danny- ok that's it, everybody get the FUCK OUT!!

Nelson- Al I think he's going to make you smell his pepperoni
Seph- (sipping soda laughing offguard, sprays some out his left nostril, which land all over the window) oops
Danny- (raises pizza paddle to Seph) LOOK YOU DID!!
Nelson- U'let's get outta hea
Alec- MY FRESHLY SQUEEZED IS ALL FUCKED UP (seems possessed by his pants)
Seph- clean that shit outside (both he and Nelson are standing waiting for Al) move stupid
Alec- (for odd reasons he snaps) NO!! YOU FUCK'N ASSHOLE I GOT THESE FOR   JEWEL-LEEEEEEEE!!
Danny- (walking over fast, with pizza spatchla in hand) WHAT'A BLACK!!U'fucking BLACKS SAY

Seph and Nelson run out the door right before Danny gets a hold of them but strangely Alec stays seated, still trying to wipe stains

Danny-YOU'OOOH,MUTHER-BATCH GET THIZ FACK OUT!! (Poking the paddle toward Alec)

31

Alec-YOUR MOTHER!!

Seph is slamming his fist on the glass

Seph-Al!Move!

Danny grabs him

Danny-I BLOW YOU!
Alec- what?
Danny-I BLOW YOU'YOU FUCK!!

Alec is finally tossed, pulling his jeans so high his
bare ankles are showing

Seph- your nuttz dude!!
Nelson-why'd you stay there?
Alec-can't you see!! (Grabbing his soda stained jeans
and stretching them out toward Nelson)
Seph-(still laughing) nuttz

Watching man slam everybody's remainders into the
trash

Seph-stop bein'a bitch for that girl
Nelson-what girl?
Seph-he likes this girl Julie in my school
Nelson- what does that have to do with his clothes?
Seph- we was all in Chess King's and she thought them jeans
looked good on him when he came out the fitt'n room
Nelson-so he bought those for that chick
Alec- Freshly squeezed nigga
Seph-cost like seventyfive dolla's
Alec -(quickly) eighty, eight zero
Nelson- EIGHT ZERO
Seph-(nostalgic) yea, that's what I said

Alec- first of all (wiping stopped) her name is Jewel-lee and second these wasn't seventyfive, they were eighty
Nelson- so...
Alec- these ain't plain lamer, these is FRESHLY SQUEEZED
Seph- you talk like orange juice'bout to squirt out them muthafucka's (coming sideways) you guys wanna go to Soundfactory tonite?
Nelson- I don't have any money
Alec- Isn't it gay night there?
Seph- its not straight nite but it ain't shootout night'niether
Nelson-sorry fella's but alls I got'sis'nickel dolla to my name
Seph- Al you want give him five and I give him five
Alec- iight, but I gotta go home and change
Nelson-thanks Al, sorry'bout the jeans
Alec-ain't mad at'cha
Seph- here (giving Nelson five bucks, turning to Al) yea you mad
Alec- (slipping a five into Nelson's hand) are you mad that girls don't want you cause you dark'skin

They walk up fiftyfifth Street toward Central Park, backs facing "Luigi's pies" which is on its way out of focus

_Scenefades

@}—'--,----------------   3

WOLF PACK FINDS BOY

Int- Picture slowly comes back in focus with Bobo and Ana walking home

It's past Midnight, they're coming back from Chinese take out

Ana- (brown bag) Bobo hold this for me (hands her brother the bag and checks her skypager)
Bobo- damn Dee, that's like the hundredth time you looked already
Ana- He said he was going to give me tickets
Bobo- Well (slightly annoyed) you'll see him in school, he IZ in your class
Ana-shush!
Bobo- (handing back the bag of food) what? It's your food
Ana- its papi's food
Bobo- you're the one he sent to get it
Ana- (almost dropping the pager as the bag is dropped right on her) watch it asshole!

As they get to their building few of the older teens from the place are hanging out on the stairway

Chez-Co- OOH, spicy mami
Ana- hi Chez
Paul- MMMMM, that smells good
Ana- its Jewish eggrolls
Paul- (sarcastically) ha,ha
Chez-Co- yoBo!Catch! (throws football)
Ana- (walking into the building) c'mon ding dong!
Bobo- Go! I'll meet you downstairs
Ana- you not supposed to be out this late

Bobo rears back to throw football ignoring his sister

35

Chez-Co- (holding his hands out for pass) we play'n football in Clinton tomorrow

Bobo-(reluctantly going upstairs, passing the guys) what time

Paul-eleven

Bobo- too early, I get up at eleven on weekend

Chez-Co- EARLY! When we was your age we used to get out at seven_AY'EM that is

Paul- you kids play too much "TECMO BOWL"

Bobo- you mean Zelda

Paul- we didn't have none of that, but we was slim, kids were OUTSIDE you FAT FUCK

Bobo- pleeeeze! All you guys do is smoke grass and walk your dogs

Chez-Co- you wanna play us then

Paul- (laughing) c'mon we'll kill'em

Bobo- Seph can outrun anybody here, and he's only fifteen

Chez-Co-that skinny Moreno you be hang'n with?

Bobo- yup'ONE FIVE

Paul- If he catches a pass over me I'll eat a box of dog biscuits

Bobo- Also Chez's sister in my room for thirty minutes ←

Chez-Co- Touch my sister and win a WET T'shirt contest (pulls out handle of something shiny)

Paul- careful CHECKS…Five'O just passed (pulling Chez's shirt down) what u give US if you lose

Bobo- I'll wax all your 'hooptees

Chez-Co- bet!

Bobo- can't wait to see slow Jew get run out

Paul- HEBREW BAALS IN YA'MOUTH FAT SPIC

Ana- (pulling Bobo away) okay say bye to these good catholics gordo

Paul- and one Jew (taps Bobo on the head with football) don't let the door hit'ya where the good lord split'ya

Chez-C0- yea and keep my sister's name unspoke SLOB

Ana and Bobo walk to the elevator where she checks her pager again

Bobo- will you stop looking at that

Ana- if you don't stop I won't let you come with me

Bobo- who wants to see Nelson naked

Ana- shut up stupid… *I like to see him*

Bobo- (teasing) dee loves a CHING CHONG KONK

Ana- SHUT UP (elevator door opens and her friend Wanda and her grandmother walk out)

Wanda- who's being so loud (smiley face)

Ana- hi Wanda

Wanda- hi Ana

Bobo- (sarcastically) hi wundah

Wanda- hi peepee boy (Wanda's grandmother walks by them whispering something to her in Spanish before walking to the front disappearing)

Ana- exactly

Wanda- whats the commotion

Bobo- Dee's in love

Ana- (sharply) Nelson's in a play across the street at that theatre and he was supposed to stop by tonight and give us tickets

Wanda- jus saw them

Ana- (startled) you did

Wanda- yea'like thirty minutes ago

Ana- where?

Wanda- we was driving back from my uncles house in Jersey and when we got out the Lincoln tunnel, I saw him and those two morenos he's always wit, hailing a cab going downtown

Ana- this late?

Wanda- you know he be going to them clubs down there

Bobo- that kid be going to clubs at midnight and I can't even toss a football around in front of the block, not fair girls

Ana- gordo you're too young to be hanging out

Bobo- Nelson's my age!

Ana- but you're not Nelson

Wanda- can't move like him either, that kid should do CLUB MTV

Ana- (lighting up her face) he be freak'n it right mami

Wanda- never seen a…. well nothing its jus… is he mixed?

Bobo- (going into elevator) I can't hear no more, move your ass Ana, Wanda your grandma is waiting in the cold, ITS COLD WAN'DUH

Wanda- Shh! (sharply, then sweetening up to Ana) bye mami happy hunting

Ana- thanks Wanda hope I catch a BIG one (they both laugh as the elevator closes)

~Scene fades

Int- Ana's elevator opens to the door of Ms.Pembells class with Lamott, Taheem, and Craig along with Hendrix staring silently at Nelson, coming into homeroom taking a seat

Ms. Pembell- I was about to mark you absent mister Obikane

Nelson- sorry Ms. Pembell, train was stuck

Lamott- EYES IS STUCK (smiling face down)

Ms. Pembell continues to count student body. Nelson takes a seat next to Rhea

Hermin- you heard 'bout my cousin

Rhea- Lamott and them robbed him after school on Friday

Nelson- that kid was your cousin?

Hermin- Yea dude

Rhea- they better watch out (looking toward Taheem and group)

Ms. Pembell- Hermin (staring at the three huddled together round Nelson's chair) Rhea?

Rhea- sorry Ms. Pembell (grabbing Hermin, going back to their seats)

Hermin- I'll see you at lunch iight

Nelson- alright...

Nelson looks around as if somethings missing

Nelson- (turning to Rhea) Ray you seen Ana?

Rhea- no, she didn't come in

Nelson- did you see her in science first period
Rhea- no you stalker

    Period bell rings and students empty out Darcy comes over
to Nelson before he exits

Darcy- did you see what happened on Friday
Nelson- no
Darcy- they jumped Mario
Nelson- who?
Darcy-Herm's cousin!
Nelson- look (almost pushing her aside) gotta go
Darcy- (grabbing him by the arm) why didn't you call me?
Nelson-what
Darcy- Remember, you was suppose to call me
Nelson- oh... something came up (pulling away) I'll see you later
Darcy- sure, I'll see you in art (looking on quietly. Nelson keeps walking)
                                                    ~Scene fades

        Int- Lunchtime, Rakim to Nelson's surprise is
standing in front of the school eating a buttered bagel

Rakim- Holy Shit! What up' Sam Spade
Nelson- you wasn't bullshitt'n
Rakim- I told you I went here (Hendrix and Lamott step out the doors, not seeing Nelson)
Lamott- OH SHIT! What up nigga (pulling over Hendrix) Yo Hen, this Craig's cousin
Hendrix- what up'what up (giving a pound)
Rakim- you West Indian (looking at Hen's red, yellow, and black belt)
Hendrix- yeh, how yuh'nuh
Rakim- Smell like Ganja in this muthafucka

Hendrix- (giving Rakim another pound) J'yah Mon! IANDI, we puff'n Ire'all'day

Taheem steps out door along with Craig, Nelson goes away

Craig- Yo Taheem, this my cuz right here
Taheem- Damn nigga you look jus like him
Hendrix- (serious tone) that little Chinese say sumthin

Rakim stares as the view fades out into a classroom setting, where Nelson is sitting next to Darcy and Kathy in art

Int- Art class, the class is divided into groups once again. Nelson is now sitting with mostly kids from his homeroom, with two from his sister class 9-221. His group is way back away from Ms. Owen's desk, last table to the back door

Darcy- so... why didn't you call me
Nelson-What?
Darcy- you was suppose to call me this weekend, what happen?
Nelson- lot of shit happened (attitude showing)
Kathy- someone looks like they got up on the wrong side of bed this morning
Nelson- (giving Kathy the bird) blow me
Kathy- eat my toto boy
Darcy- you could'a come ova (smiling). My dad went to Vegas
Nelson- Your dad was in Vegas! (Not seeing Kathy roll her eyes, as his ill attitude turns to curiosity)
Darcy- yea, he's a cooler...
Nelson- A cooler! What's that?
Darcy- you ever see in the movies when a guy's in a casino making crazy money, and he keeps winning
Nelson-yea
Darcy- that would never happen in real life
Nelson- (cutting her off) your dad's a bouncer

40

Darcy- (looking as if Nelson should know better) nooooo, you can't kick someone out jus'cuz their hittin their numba's
Nelson- oh
Darcy- my dad comes over and stands there

Nelson- what?
Darcy- he stands there and all of a sudden the winning guy starts losing
Nelson- losing? (Kathy is now almost touching her ears with her pursed lips, as she can't believe Nelson going for it)
Darcy- well he's a natural jinx
Nelson- whoa (wide eyed)
Darcy- I'm serious, when a player gets on a roll, which rarely happens but it does every once in a blue
Kathy- (sarcastically) it's called cheat'n
Darcy- Nah! People can get lucky sometimes, lobsters roll'
Kathy- and let me guess...
Darcy- that's right, they call my dad down and he goes Cools'em off
Nelson- (believing whole heartedly) crazy (Kathy sighing heavily)
Kathy- OK, I'm gonna go change the water cup now (getting up, walking away) becareful Nelson you don't step into bullshit
Nelson- (attitude disappearing) you know I did call you last night
Darcy- no you didn't (girlyface)
Nelson- I did but the fuck'n phone was off, I even called the operator and she was like, the number is correct but the line was disconnected
Darcy- OH! I was watching re-runs of "I dream of Genie"
Nelson- you like old TV?
Darcy- I love it, especially when she leans on the Major (she says the last part with lazy Italian eyes, her almond lids targeting Nelsons pupil)
Nelson- (feeling deep emotion from Darcy's stare, he forgets himself) move closer
Darcy- (pushing her chair right next to his) what's up (in lite tone)

Nelson rubs outside her jeans under the desk

Darcy- (whispering) little lower (She takes her hand and guides his fingers)
Nelson- I know what I'm doing
Darcy- (smiling) jus trying to help
Nelson- I don't need it (pushing hard)
Darcy- OW, easy (still whispering) stop!
Nelson- alright I'll be easy
Dannielle- no look (Kathy staring, walking toward them)
Nelson- shit
Kathy- (banging the cup down, water splashing everywhere) well, well, well, what a difference a trip to the sink makes
Darcy- you wanna smell his fingers Kathy
Kathy- you nasty
Nelson- (looking pissed) why you have to sit here if you see… you know…
Kathy- cause I can't sit nowhere else. Anyway if you wanna keep doing what you wuz doin go head, don't let me bother you, it's not like I'm'a be stare'n at your toto mami (Darcy starts to rub Nelson through his pants going up and down. Kathy turns away to ignore them)

Period bell rings. Darcy kisses Nelson on the cheek and runs off

Darcy- that was nice… I'll see you tomorrow, I'm cutting eighth
Nelson- bye
Darcy- bye cutie

Nelson walks toward the front door to give in his painting

Taheem and Hendrix is there packing up their group table

42

Hendrix hears Nelson and turns to him, but stays
quiet, so does Taheem

Nelson- here I finished this, where should I put it
Ms. Owen- (giving him a woodclip) hang it next to the window
(a clothe string lines the window sill, Nelson clicks it on, then
turns to a staring Taheem and Hendrix still silent)
Nelson- bye Ms. Owen (Taheem stares all the way till he's out
the door)

~Scene fades

Int- History, Mr. Sapt's class, Rhea and Hermin are sitting
together, whispering, while the class is reading in silence.
Nelson in the background, along with Hendrix, Taheem, Craig
sitting next to him

Rhea- don't look now, but Nelson's got the best seat in'hizzy
Hermin- if they fuck with him (looking right past Reah to the
back) I'm gonna fight
Reah- are you crazy Hermin
Hermin- that's my friend sitting over there'ray
Rhea- you only met him this year Herm (cynical stare) get like,
for' real
Hermin- oh it's gonna get REAL, if they start (Rhea could see
he *really* means it)
Rhea- is this cause of Mario (Herm stays quiet)

Rhea is not pleased with Hermin's choice of friends but
she's very pleased with the Graffiti artwork that she's putting
away in her bag

Rhea- thanks for the... uh (searching for proper term as
she stares at the work of art Hermin just gave her)
Hermin- it's called a "Burner"
Reah- yea, the'burner (slight tint of pink on her face)

Period bell goes off. Nelson quietly packs and waits for Hermin as Taheem and his group leave

Reah- (kisses Hermin exiting) here Herm, your BLOOD brother is waiting for you!

Hermin- (coming over unlike himself) Nelson, those guys didn't say anything stupid to you, did they
Nelson- nah
Hermin- at all
Nelson- zilch, zero
Hermin- you think they try'n to catch you off guard
Nelson- I don't know, go figure
Hermin- hey (taking a large black binder out his green army bag)
Nelson- (Hermin opens black binder and hands him a mini-poster sized burner of his name "Nelly'Nel") HOLY SHIT!
Mr. Sapt- Nelson, I'm not Christian, but I do believe that's inappropriate grammer in both Hebrew and Jen'tilly
Nelson- sorry Mr. S, I was just complimenting my Eastern European compatriot about his fine... (he's cut off by the teacher)
Mr. Sapt- Nelson (Looking superior) Get out (curtly)
Hermin- (laughing) let's go
Nelson- (holding painting) THIS LOOKS PRICELESS
Hermin- (walking out with Nelson) nah, *this* is nutt'n. You should see my brothers stuff (eye's lighting up) He's like the "Bob Ross" of 'Astoria
Nelson- yeah well, I'm a put it up
Hermin- how bout' teach me some steps and we'll call it even (Hermin doing a silly move)
Nelson- it's gonna take alot of work
Hermin- oh excuse me, MISTER Asian dance master
Nelson- oh exuse me, mister Slavic'Vango
Hermin- and like, you Japs are any better
Nelson- lucky I'm in good mood bout this painting
Hermin-Burner

Nelson- whateva (Hermin laughs)   ~SC End

Int~ Tanya outside after school speaking to Nelson

Tanya- I'm telling you I didn't see her all day, and she didn't call me last night, telling me if she was going to cut
Nelson- did she call you anytime in the weekend sounding pissed at me
Tanya- (looking as if she's going to explode) ay, ca'brong! I'm telling you I didn't hear, see, or talk to Ana since Friday comprende Nell-San!
Nelson- (looking confused) where could she be?
Tanya- why are you so ON IT?
Nelson- I was suppose'tuh give her tickets to...
Tanya- that play she keeps telling me about
Nelson- she told you'bout my play?
Tanya- (not liking Nelson happy) don't get too excited papi, she told me about the thong you have to wear, it's a joke bout'u
Nelson- well if she calls you...
Tanya- I know, I know, I'll tell her you're looking for her
Nelson- thanks mami
Tanya- don't call me mami (turning and walking away) you don't know me like that
Nelson- (waiting til Tanya's out of earshot) thank god for that

A lady with Bible pamphlets passes by and hands him a flyer with Reinhold Niebuhr's serenity prayer on it. He waits till she's out of view then drops it. The pamphlet is zoomed in on, gliding down. On the picture there's two men on a ladder talking, the view transforms the two men painted into a real life shot of Seph and Alec in discussion, with Nelson in the staircase of his building

Alec- So between me and Seph there's real difference in blood?
Nelson- well. (pause) Yeah, I mean look at your face and color, it's much different then Seph's

45

Seph- but we're both Black

Nelson- yea, but, you can tell Al is mixed

Seph- there's mixed Chinese

Nelson- not as much as mixed Blacks

Alec- I bet theres a lot of mixed Asians (tilts head) you jus don't hear about it

Nelson- I'm not saying there isn't any. But black dudes sleep wit'all different chicks (pause) so lot of girls have mixed kids here

Seph- so what's the difference between Chinese, Japanese, and Korean?

Nelson- prolly...nothing

Seph- you know, I know this Chinese kid in one O four (pause) and he'd prolly fight you if he heard that

Alec- who Eric? (unbelieving) get the fuck outta here! Nelson would kill Eric

Seph- yo Eric know's that shit yo (doing a weird martial arts hand gesture)

Nelson- I think that's all hype

Seph- WHAT! THAT NIGGA WILL FLIP YAH, FLIP YOU FOR REAL

Alec- I seen them five O one kid's tax that nigga's beeper, all he was flip'n was quarters in lunch, call'n his moms and shit to come get him

Seph- CHARGED!

Alec- word is bond

Seph- (quickly twice) word is bond CHARGED-BULLSHIT!

Nelson- (curious) who are these "five O one" kids you keep mentioning

Alec- hoodlums, a gang...

Seph- (talking over Alec) they ain't no gang (states case to Nelson) these kids is MAD BOOTY

Alec- nah yo, some them dudes is crazy

Seph- how much you wanna bet, any'a those kids fuck wit me, I'm gonna FLIP THEM, ALL'THEM, FLIP'EM FO'REAL

Alec- ok, ok, you big gorilla nigga, so NELSON, getting back to the original point, you really don't see a difference between Chinese, Korean and all that

Nelson- well, we all look the same don't we, I mean (Nelson stretches his eyes out slanted) we all have the same thing

Alec- yea but, look how dark you are. Most Chinese are like yellow almost

Seph- first of all he ain't Chinese, he Japanese, it's a whole other country, just incase you didn't know, bruh-DA

Alec- come on, you mess with them Chinese food chinks all the time, so don't lie!

Seph- yea but they ain't Japanese nigga, they is CHINESE

Nelson- what's the difference

Alec- (smiling gratifyingly) that's what I'm say'n

Seph- dude, you shouldn't say that

Nelson- why not

Seph- cause you ain't the same dude, y'all have a whole different style yo I'm serious

Alec- and you know this because... (waiting for response)

Seph- my dad was there after he came back from Vietnam (pause) and from what he told me, (sincerely) they was cool peoples

Nelson- (Irritated) MINTS, made in Japan COOL (sarcasm)

Alec- (laughing) COX! (Lunges to slap Seph on the head)

Seph- touch me and see what happens, fuck'n dreadlock

Nelson- all's right fella's take it easy (stepping inbetween)

Alec- CHILL, what the fuck, you aint Chinese! It's not like I'm calling you a MOO'LEE

Nelson- Al is right, what's the big deal

Seph- (trying to reason) Nelson you know what you sound like... a sell out

Nelson-WHAT

Seph- sell out, it means turncoat, Judas, Benidict Arnold

Alec- yo, I'm outta hea (grabbing his coat off the banister) lata Nel (gives Nelson a pound and a shoulder, but ignores Seph)

Seph- later bitch (Al keeps walking)

Alec leaves, slamming door hard

Nelson- what is your malfunction!

Seph- you need' talk to my pops

Nelson- I'm tired of it bro, why do you make a fight all the time?

Seph- (as if he's talking to himself) you know Al is only one fourth black right

Nelson- and?

Seph- his dad's Italian, *and* his mom is half black, she mad light skin

Nelson- So, he's still Al!

Seph- yo his dad talks about you around his friends at that deli he works at, talking all this racist shit about Asians you wouldn't even know Holmes. They be laughing for hours, and I know that if I wasn't there playing video games infront of them, they'd have something to say about me too

Nelson- yea, but its not like Al feel's that way

Seph- HE BE LAUGH'N RIGHT WITH THEM DUDES

Nelson-WHAT?

Seph- when they be talk'n bout you, (pause) he blends right in wit them, laughing and shit

Nelson- whats he suppose'tah do, fight his dad's boss and get'em fired

Seph- well you better know (eyes raised) cause, he be scream'n on you

Nelson- if Alec is racist, why does his dad let me come over, and treat me to food and movies

Seph- I'm not saying their Klu-Klux-Klan racist, I'm saying that, in their eyes you not equal to them, doesn't that bother you?

Nelson- maybe, but...

Suddenly a shrilling voice bombards the hallway

Shiela- SEPH

Seph-MOMMY!

Sheila- I know you not in that staircase talking with that little fucker

Seph- Yo I gotta go get some shit for my moms at the Red Apple, you wanna come wit'me

Nelson- k

Seph- what you doin for Thanksgiving

Nelson- eating at your place

Seph- (grabs him in headlock playfully) My Nigga

They both rush downstairs

_End scene

{Note}

1 The overuse of the word "Nigga" was prevelant towards the late 80's as a more accepted term even outside African American linguistics. I never added the word to my vocabulary, not because of the political aspect of it but for the plain reason, it just never rolled off my tongue.

2 In the past scene Alec and Seph discuss Asian countries as separate cultures. Unfortunately China is spoken of in less flattering fashion than Japan. But in my best memory, I've never took it as an insult to be mistaken for Chinese as other Asians have always hollered "I'm Korean" or "I am Phillipino" "Native North, Central, and South American". In my math it always added up that the first people that had these facial features were from China. Now I know that Philipino's have European blood from conquest and that Japanese have traces of Caucasian DNA from the Siberian pass *Ice Age (beards, chest hair) so I give certain Asian countries their two cents in claims of not being completely Mongoloid. But it cannot be overlooked, that if there is a beginning for the physical make up of the Asian demographic it must be China, from the bones of thee undeniable Peking man.

3 Seph was always fiery and passionate growing up. But sometimes I thought he could have held back a bit. Funny that over time I became an actor, for out of us... the more dramatic was clearly not me.

49

Int- Alec is walking up a windy fiftysixth street when he runs into Cristian Polysevski. Trees bend and papers fly around when they talk

Cris- FOOTBALL HEAD!
Alec-WHITE CHOCOLATE!
Cris- I had to drop by my moms to pick up my Super Nintendo
Alec- that's right, you live wit ya moms only on weekends right
Cris- (rushing) yea, yea, did you see Ana?
Alec- not today
Cris- blind or sumthin she just came this way, should'a seen her
Alec- what you mean
Cris- half her face is purple
Alec- what?
Cris- I tried to talk to her, but she jus said hi, and left like it was an emergency
Alec- think Nelson knows what happened
Cris- maybe, she's always with that little bastard, speak'n of Yoshi, if you see'm, tell him to drop by on Friday, I got sumth'n to show'em
Alec- alright (pause) she looked hit up?
Cris- yea dude (giving Alec a high five) I know you probably want to talk bout it, but (raises brown paper bag he's holding) gotta go
Alec- I understand yo, private school ain't cheap, you prolly make sure you get your moneys worth and study'study
Cris- not that at all, I just gotta get these sandwiches from Carnegie to my pops
Alec- you ain't gonna offer me
Cris- No offer, DESERT STORM sandwiches dude (walking off) hope everything is cool with Ana
Alec- yea, me too (they part) later
Cris- later'later (repeats) LATER!

Cristian walks off with the back of his sweater showing a large number four emblazoned on it, fading out of view into the next scene, which opens on a stone number four engraved on a building near Oxford junior high

   Int- Lamott, Taheem and Craig are eating bagels
sitting on the stoop

Lamott- I wanna' fuck that little Mexican bitch
Craig- who Liza
Lamott- nah, not her yo, that girl Ana always be around
Craig- Melissa
Lamott- NAH man! That chick wit the crooked nose and shit
Craig-Kathy…
Taheem-(cutting off Craig) Tanya
Lamott-YEA! That bitch

   Group of eighth graders, clearly looking up to the
ninth graders, come around trying to impress Taheem and
friends. Three of the eighth graders step up

Robert 8th grader- yo, Lamott (flexing his biceps) think I
could get as big as you
Jaime 8th grader- damn you little spic! (Smiling at Lamott)
Tell Mini-mouse he can swing from ya' nuttz
Lamott- both of y'all could swing
Craig- (pointing at Robert, then Jaime) he got two balls, one
for each of you
Taheem- (blasting out) NUTTZ IN YA MOUTH LIKE…
SQUIRRELS!!
Cashmeer8th grader- yeah, hairy nuttz in them
muthafucka's! (Pushing Jaime)
Lamott- (smirking) while they swing'n on deez, you can
suckee'suckee
Jaime 8th grader- (slapping Cashmeer on back of his neck)
AHHHHH! SUCK HIS DICK BOY!
Robert8th grader- (running into Cashmeer) yeah suck'dick!
Cashmeer 8th grader- (throwing Robert to the ground)
where your muscle froggy!
Robert 8th grader- get off me!

Suddenly four to five suspicious looking white teens are on the corner of seventy eighth street

Rakim- Craig! Why didn't you wait for me?
Craig- I thought you was going to be in there forever
Taheem- what he ask you?
Rakim- same shit (looking up to the sky) why I was in Jew'Vee,
if I did somethin' violent or hurt someone
Lamott- look at these niggas (Robert pulls out a combination
lock from his jacket)

Eighth graders are getting annoying

Cashmeer 8th grader- (dodging a swing of padlock and fist,
getting off the top of Robert) chill that's a lock!
Robert 8th grader- (finds Lamott staring at him) I told you bout
fuck'n wit me right bitch! (Hoping he's impressed) I don't play
that bitch! (throws the padlock from the seat of his pants, missing
badly, as the padlock goes over a ducking head through a window
of the first floor tenement)

Instantly a man comes out, ripped jeans and a
lady with blonde hair

Man- What the FUCK! (looks at all the kids) WHO DID THIS?

Everybody gets off the stoop

Man- (looking at Craig) you did this?
Craig- no
Man- Then why you look'n at me?
Craig- (looking at Rakim then Taheem, then back to the man)
look why don't you go back inside, nobody broke your SHIT
Man- What the fuck you said
Rakim- I think what my cousin is trying to say is, just
because we're Black didn't mean we broke glass (looking
over at Robert) why don't you ask one them

52

Man- I'm asking NOTHING OK (staring dead at Rakim, then Craig, and Lamott) just get off my property!

Lamott, Taheem, eighth graders, all stand there oddly, when Nelson walks quietly alone past them, stopping at the broken glass holding a coke bottle

Man- DID YOU HEAR WHAT I SAID (slinging the padlock down)
Lady blonde- (seeing that the kids are stalemate) look just go, we're not calling the cops or anything (very nicely)
Robert 8th grader- that's my GYM PAD LOCK
Man- WHAT! (Immediately runs inside, then back out in a flash with giant boat paddle in hand)

Nelson looks back to the dozen or so white kids he passed and notices that they are beginning to walk up

Man- (stomping fast toward a retreating Robert) COME HERE (shirt now off, revealing tattoo's of native American art, and band out of hair, wind blowing black strands around his gaunt face) I don't care about your stinking LOCK... (looking at the group of eighth graders now silent and all backing away)
Lady blonde- Steve! (Nervously) get inside (picking up his shirt and hairband) the police!
Steve- (walks through Taheem, Craig, and Lamott) Watch it Sandra, you got slippers, go back
Lamott- told you we ain't do it
Steve- (Ignoring Lamott) let's go bay, you didn't cut your foot on any glass did you
Lamott- (moving out the way, as Steve pulls Sandra inside and slams the door) Yo where that punk nigga Robert at

Nelson walks up to Rakim gesturing

Craig- (running up from behind, right into Nelson's grill) WHAT THE FUCK HE WANT!
Rakim- yo chill cuz, LOOK (backs Craig off, points finger)

Craig looks up to see a group of White teens
walking straight toward them

Taheem- come on (picks up Roberts padlock) lets go back

Taheem's group and eigth graders begin to walk

The group of white teens follow

Rakim- Nelson (long silent stare by Rakim
followed by an awkward smile) you wit'us

Craig, Lamott, and Taheem turn at this

Nelson-(looking at the strange boys following them, picking
bottles out of garbage bins and bricks from the floor amongst
other things, weighing the consequences in his mind, which is
developing around his brow, visible now to all, raises his eyes
to Ra and whispers through the Fall wind) *yea*

A black ring forms around the screen blacking everything
out, zeroing down on Nelson's face. The ring opens up again
after a moment with Nelson in the doorway of Ox's auditorium,
sporting a shiner

Nelson walks in, as Taheem, Lamott, Rakim, and Craig
are all being detained, waiting for questioning

Nelson- (coming over to sit next to Rakim) hey Ra

Rakim and the rest stay silent, while Nelson sits. After a
minute or so, he takes their quiet to be a sign of unwant and rises
up to move away

Lamott- (screaming) YO"TOO'WONG FOO"SITDOWN!!

Rakim- (grabbing Nelson in a bear hug from the back, then calling out to the rest) I told you bout' this kid… RIGHT!

Craig- here (handing Nelson an icepack) keep that shit from blow'n up (pointing at his eye)
Taheem- (slowly walks over) HEY! (everyone goes mute to listen) does a Chinese girl pussy go like this (index finger going up and down) or like this (index finger going left to right)

      Everyone laughs, including Nelson, while Hendrix Crew and his brothers stroll in

Hendrix- Yo what the fuck so funny (smiling looking over) This rude boy, JaPAN style, GOT heart like Judah fight like LION
Dante- (looking at Rakim) RAKIM, you got no eye blud'clot (frustrated) you no see dem olive boys all ova' me' dread!
Rakim- I had that big "ROCKY FOUR" Drago look'n nigga swing'n on me (matter a factly)
Ferno- (laughing at Dante) wha'you give for saving your life
Dante- only Jesus saves
Ferno- Bati'bwa
Dante- no problem

      The dean Levi and principle Rosebaum both walk in with two security guards and an officer

Dean Levi- BACK IN MY DAY, THEY'D GIVE YA' ALL A SWIFT KICK IN THE NUT JUST FOR HAVING THOSE FACES ON (looking over at Hendrix) BUT SINCE IT'S THE NINETY'S (then Nelson) DEFINITLY THE NINETIES, ALL WE'S CAN DO IS GIVE YOU'S DETENTION TILL THE END OF THE WEEK!

Mr Rosebaum- There are few of you, who I will be speaking to before you go home (looking at Taheem and Lamott) the rest leave

Like sixth sense, Lamott and Taheem pick up their things and walk right over to the security guards. Everyone else pauses

Dean Levi- you heard the man (now panning the rest) SCRAM

The students leave, all giving a pound to the two standing next to the guards and the cop. Nelson is last to get out

Nelson- (watching Ferno give a quick pound to Taheem then jet out, Nelson does the same) lata
Taheem-YO (grabs Nelson)
Nelson- (mute)
Taheem- thanks
Nelson- (best he can do) okay

_EndScene

*   *

@}—'--,----------------4

KGBoys

Int- Ana is walking out Blimpie's, when from the corner of her eye she spots Nelson standing across the street. She rushes back into the sandwich shop and goes straight to the bathroom, with bags of food and all. She waits inside a few moments then opens the door, only to see Nelson sitting at the table right in front of her, smiling first then turning into a twisted face of worry

Nelson- (running up) WHAT HAPPENED?
Ana- (looking down, walking fast) I can't talk…
Nelson- (grabs, sits her down) Ana!
Ana- look I fell ok
Nelson- Fell? (sighing) on both sides of your face
Ana- (tongue in cheek) you wouldn't know about it
Nelson- Ana! (soft spoken) *talk to me*
Ana- I tried to stop my dad…
Nelson- (fills in rest) from beating your mom
Ana- (startled) yea

*Time slows down as boy and girl open a chapter of their lives to one another, revealing things most people keep to themselves

Nelson- its jus'insults from my dad. Your thing is physical, mine sticks and stones love
Ana- (misty look) how do you know?
Nelson- at least your dad works (deep breath, looking away) shit my pops talks and sleeps all day
Ana- but (looking up) you live here
Nelson- Ann, I ain't rich, spoiled, or well off, my dad moved here when it was cheap, now they can't get him out (changing up) is ding-dong and your mom alright?
Ana- I'm the only one that got hit
Nelson- you must've stuck up for everybody, sorry
Ana- nah (pause) usually if he hits something really hard a few times he calms down, (shrugs her shoulder) this time it just happened to be me

Ana- not your fault my dad's a fuck'n coward

   A cop walks past them into the restroom looking at
Nelson suspiciously

Ana- where's your mom?
Nelson- mom…
Ana- your madre, you know MOTHER? never seen her
Nelson- Oh, left when I was (puts his hand low off the table)
Ana- you don't see her
Nelson- she left when I was six and that was it
Ana- maybe if she was here you wouldn't be going through this
Nelson- nah (getting up) she's worse then my dad (whipping out
Blimpie's gift card Joel gave him) want'a'share a hot chocolate?
Ana- (pointing at her sandwich bags) ding'dong'll start crying if I
don't get his cheese combos to him before Batman comes on
Nelson- I thought that show only comes on Sunday
Ana- his stupid friend records it (looking up) "In LivingColor"
"Married with children"
Nelson- you forgot "Seinfeld"
Ana- ay, please, don't get me started
Nelson- (smiling) here this might come in handy (offers cocoa
butter)
Ana- (surprised) I didn't know Asians used that
Nelson- we don't, Taheem gave this to me…
Ana-Taheem?
Nelson- long story

   Ana looks as if she's about to ask a thousand questions

Nelson- it's best for everybody if we just hear your case now
Ana- but… (cut off)
Nelson- (puts a finger to her lips) trus me

   Ana simmers down reluctantly

Ana- K, but you better tell me bout'it

Nelson- promise

Ana- (grinning) yea, I bet (changing up) why didn't you get me those tickets I asked for?

Nelson- after the show Seph and Al dragged me out…

Ana- to a club

Nelson- yea (oddly) how'd you know?

Ana- better watch out (pokes Nelsons chest) I got eyes and ears around here

Nelson- (playfully) rite

Ana- so when will I have them

Nelson- Have what?

Ana- tickets Einstien

Nelson- (jumping into his bookbag) OH yea! (Pulling out three stiff lamenated strips) these are for Wednesday night, their kind of on the side but that was the best I could do (hands passes)

She stares at the tickets, head down

Ana- their so pretty (tranced out)

Nelson- do you want me to carry the soda's for you?

Ana- OH!, I mean, no, I can… well thanks (looking out of place, talking fast) I'll be there at (staring at the passes) nine thirty

Nelson- want me to stick this in your pocket (flashing cocoa butter)

Ana- I got tubs of that in my house, did you forget I'm half PR Nelson

Nelson- right

Ana- thanks (Nelson can't help but look at her shirt which says "Let me be your angel")

They walk down the block together till Nelson reaches his lobby where Joel the doorman is waiting

Joel- Hi mami (wide grin)

Nelson- (looks at Joel till he knows not to google, then turns back to Ana) bye

Ana- bye (kisses Nelson on the cheek)

Nelson watches her walk down the corner, passing Southerly pharmacy, then heads in

Joel- Awwwwww, isn't that sweet
Nelson- comedian, open the door
Joel- sure thing Mr.Sensitive (notices swollen eye) "DIABLO"

Lobby door closes in flash of darkness

_End Scene

Int- Alec is with Seph on the roof

Seph- Joel told me Nel had a black eye
Alec- Joel?
Seph- Joel, bellboy, you know doorman
Alec- wow, a living afro-thesarus
Seph- blow me, he said when Nelson came by he was talk'n to Ana, then when he turned he saw a red mark on his eye, puffy
Alec- you know her face is fucked up too
Seph- Ana?
Alec- I ran into Cris yesterday when I left y'all, and he told me Ann's face was all beat down
Seph- Joel didn't say nutth'n about Ana'tho
Alec- maybe he didn't see her
Seph- I just told you he did
Alec- did Joel say Nel looked pissed
Seph- what, you think Nelson did that
Alec- maybe they argued
Seph- I said Joel told me HE had a black eye (annoyed) not Ana
Alec- well, we'll know when he gets here

Seph- what time is it

Alec- (looking up at the Mony clock) six

Seph- that nigga… (buttoning up, from the wind)
He always' late!

Alec- so Joel said he was all fucked up

Seph- bet he's exaggerating

Alec- why would he lie?

Seph- exaggerate not lie

Alec- what's the difference?

Nelson comes through the rooftop exit

Seph- Big Nel!

Alec- WHERES MY BEEF'N BROCCOLI!

Nelson- quiet asshole! (Pointing to his head) I don't feel good

Seph- whoa! What happened?

Alec- That shit is black like shit yo

Seph- Shit is brown too, iight

Nelson- I got into some shit today (rubbing his forehead)

Seph- That Taheem nigga you was tell'n Ra about

Nelson- yup (long silence, looking out over Hells Kitchen into the Hudson)

Seph- I knew you was in for it after what Ra said in Luigi's

Nelson- fella's I think I jus fell'inta the Twilight zone

Alec-huh

Nelson- some kids came to fight'em (looks up) and I fought

Seph-WHAT?

Nelson- guess which side I swung for (looks up again)

Alec- (by Nelson's expression Alec already knows) *the Blacks*

Nelson-Rakim really is family with that Craig kid

Seph- And you lucky he is, now you get a pass from Craig

Nelson- you could say that again. Hate that guy too!

Seph- and you fought for him? Why

Nelson- long story

Seph- you gonna tell us what happened bruh'a man

Nelson- if you can keep your mouth shut, I will!
(Rubbing his head)

Alec- yea, nigga (grinning) shut up
Seph- Toss yo skinny ass off this roof (grabbing the fence, shaking it)

Nelson begins to speak, as the camera shot dives under Seph's feet, blanking out the scene for moment then back up into a flashback of the rumble that took place in the schoolyard earlier

Lamott- ONLY WARRIORS CAN STAY!

There's a group of eighth graders standing in the middle of the schoolyard, backing away into school doors, prepared to run

Craig- Lamott...
Lamott- what?
Craig- have some them little nigga's stay, we need heads
Lamott- Fuck them faggots
Craig- but theres only eight of us (looking around at ninth graders infront of school grounds)
Rakim- here they come

The gang of White teens come storming in, all sorts of things in their hands, one steps to the forefront and shatters a bottle on the concrete. They all look physically fit. He seems to be the leader, if there is one

Otto- WHICH OF YOU HAS MY BROTHERS WATCH!! (He does not look happy) if you give it back we leave no question

There are eleven in all, as they focus on Taheem and friends. Some look over at Nelson in confusion, then stare again into the black kids, mostly the bigger ones, which all happen to be in Nelson's class, except for, Rakim

63

Lamott- I told you they was pussy

Lamott referring to eighth graders who acted out to impress the older teens, only to flee inside the school, when danger showed up

Craig- look, no one here has anything from your brother

Mario's brother, Eska, steps up

Eska- WHATS'THAT (pointing at Ferno's wrist)
Otto- look we came from Astoria Queens (looking right and left to his band of brothers) and we didn't come all this, to leave with nothing (staring at Ferno)
Hendrix- I bought him clock'mon (twisting his dreads)

Another white teen steps into view, this one is bigger then everyone on the field except for Lamott, who is as brawny, but shorter.

Klitchko- LIAR!

He runs at Rakim, throws him down quick and starts to pummel his face. Violence explodes on the playground of the Junior High

Taheem- (grabs Nelson) stay on my left (Nelson is dazed) ON MY LEFT BOY! (Taheem runs past everyone in deep brawl and from his pocket, hits Klitchko on the neck with the padlock Robert threw through Native's window)

Klitchko- (bleeding from the neck, gets off a lost Rakim) FUCK'NNIGGER! (smiling)
Taheem-(calm) fight me

Nelson helps up Rakim, who almost falls again

Rakim- look (pointing at shorter thugs beating on Dante) go help him
Nelson- (heart pounding) k

Nelson runs fast he can past a laughing Lamott who is headbutting a white teen lifeless on the floor, and without consciousness RAMS right into Ferno, Hendrix other brother

Ferno- Damn Bloodclut! (cools himself seeing that he was going to help Dante) come on

Ferno swings wildly at two of the three kids but the third is still punching his brother in the face. Nelson pulls the kids hair with both hands insanely, and yanks him off. Nelson looks down and see's Dante wrecked, unable to stand, he is completely out his senses, drooling out his mouth, splicing down his cheek

Dimitri- (connects with a running fist which staggers Nelson) CHINESE!CHINESE!CHINESE! (Swings again but misses badly, off balance. He doesn't gain his center quick enough, for Nelson cocks back and punches him right in the Mouth)

Dimitri takes a knee grabbing his face with two hands

Nelson- fuck you call'n Chinese, the name's ADOLPH, as in HITLER

All fighters stop, turn right to him. Silence and idleness are causing fear to dwell on everyone. There are feint sounds of sirens in the distance

Lamott- (unable to move, breaks the tension) FIVE O!! (Runs to Taheem who is standing man up with Klitchko, both bloody and panting) COME ON NIGGA'! 'FIVE'O!!

Sirens and whistles of police cars echo through the alley, as students' book into school doors and Russians jet out

Some of the kids take cheap'hits on the way out, Nelson
being victim to one

Taheem-NELSON!

Klitchko- HEY LOOK (knockout shot)

Taheem runs to Nelson who's struggling to keep his
legs under him

Taheem- FUCK!! I told you to stay CLOSE! (dragging him
out, feet scraping the floor) I got you homie, we gon'make' it
(blue and red lights, including wailing sounds of emergency are
flooding the school yard. Walkie-talkie's could be heard
nasaling everywhere) we gon'make it…

Camera zooms in on Nelson's sneaker digging
through the pavement, rolling over concrete, broken glass,
and gravel slipping into the present

Back to the future

He lays two elbows on the fence of his roof, sunlight
beginning to fade into a dark blue sky, city lights sparkling
up all around, as he looks out over the Hudson.

Seph- (low voice) you alright
Nelson- I'm ok, kind'a scared that's all
Seph- you think them nigga's is comin'back?
Nelson- I would say yea, they looked pissed
Alec- if you want (putting a hand over Nelsons right shoulder) I
could talk to my boy Gilky…
Seph- (Tossing Alec's hand off) PLEASE, don't bring up them
five-O-one's!
Alec- WHAT THE FUCK, I'm trying to back yoshi up
Seph- he got people already! (Shaking his head) reliables!
Alec- lick deez eye'a'bull nutz
Seph- (Ignoring Al) what difference day makes

66

Nelson- (Turns to Seph) huh?

Seph- (laughing, bear hugging Nelson, and raising him chanting the "Twilight Zone" theme) YOU HAVE NOW JUST ENTERED (looking crazy) THE TWILIGHT ZONE!

Nelson- my head is ring'n big mouth

Seph- Oh get on wit'it (poking his ribs) you'll live

Alec- oh shit look (pointing to the building adjacent to them, a man and woman's having sex)

Nelson- what?

Alec- you don't see them fucking? (taking binoculars out his pack)

Seph-Stop lyin

Alec- I'm serious! Look! (points four floors down)

Seph-where?

Nelson- follow'my finger (tracing toward the window where sex is taking place)

Seph-Whoa!

Nelson- (quickly) Al, give me your binoculars

Alec- no

Seph- fuck you carry'n around binoculars for you peep'n Tom (hears an orgasmic squeal burst from that side) Quick gimme binoculars

Alec-same answer no

Seph- you know who that looks like

Alec- your moms

Seph- my moms ain't twelve, idiot (snatching binoculars)

Alec- who the fuck are you talking about?

Seph- (looking through) wait (mouth slowly opened) Holy crap!

Nelson- Give me those shits (snatches binoculars, as Seph turns to Alec)

Seph- You tell'n me all the time you was staring, you couldn't tell who she was!?

Nelson-OH SHIT! That's Chez-Co's sister!

Alec-WHAT? (Snatching the binoculars back)

Seph- you need glasses nigga

Alec- fuck me! It is (another scream yelps out) that nigga bang'n her looks mad old' tho

Seph- Nigga nope, JEW yes and the Jew bangin her is the owner of the pharmacy downstairs (SOUTHERLY'S)
Nelson-beck?
Alec- STEINBECK!
Nelson- ain't he like sixty
Alec- for a ol'nigga, he got a big DICK
Seph- Damn you be look'n at BIG dicks and shit
Nelson- (hearing a scream coming right from the window, as does Seph) she sound like…
Alec- She look like she gonna cry, her legs is kick'n mad crazy
Seph- someone should'a told that bitch bout fuck'n grown ass men
Nelson- (laughing) Chez treats that guy like he's the pope of the Kitchen
Seph- (doing impression) I know, I know, Mr. Beck. I know these are bad for me, just give me a few weeks and I'll be a quitter
Nelson-(doing Stienbeck impersonation) YEA'you do that ya'fuck'n spic! And tell your dirty little sister to come by and pick these FUCK'N CHEESEBALLZ!
Seph- (head kicked sideways, snapping a finger, and planting his feet) YOU GOT IT SENOR'WHY-TEEE!
Nelson- you getting uppity wit me CooChi Fri-TOE's!
Seph-NO, NO papi'chupa me'

Nelson pulls out an imaginary whip and starts snapping at Seph while Seph mimics a Ricky Ricardo accent, when out of the blue Al breaks the antics

Alec- oh no
Nelson-what?
Alec- she swallowed it (Big Stein cumms in her mouth)
Seph-What! (snatching back the binoculars)

Seph-   Chez would kill that nigga if he saw this

Alec- didn't he stab a dude before for goin out with Ellen?
Seph- he would sew that nigga's asshole up (giggling) and keep

feeding him, and feeding him

Alec- (out of nowhere) you know what we gotta do right

Nelson- what, tell Chez his sisters gett'n the ol' salami

Alec- NO! (looking up) am I the only one who thinks around here I'm gonna record that shit on my camcord

Nelson- (being serious) Look, I know we all don't like Chez-Co, but still, that's his little sister

Seph- (sarcastic tone) yea perverts his SISTA. Plus don't all your tapes have Nel dance'n in'em   ←

Alec- No you asshole! (snatching back his goggles) I'm gonna record it and send a tape mysteriously enveloped to the pharmacy

Nelson- Your gonna do what?

Alec- then I'm going to write a note telling him if he don't give me whatever I want every time I go in that muthafucka (slapping his hand on the safety fence) WHOOMP! Jigs up

Seph- Tape goes to Chez-co

Alec- tape goes to Chez-co

Nelson- I like it (grinning mischievously)

Seph- the sun shines even a dog's ass (looking evil) LET'S DO IT

_Scene End__

{Note}

1 Taheem's company is numerous so here is a list

Taheem, Lamott, Rakim, Craig, Hendrix, Dante, Ferno

Later on they begin to call themselves "TA7" (The Amazing Seven)

Lamott was tagged "Arnold" for his body building physique

Taheem "Genius" for he was the smartest of the group

Rakim and Craig were tagged "Black Irish" cousins that hailed from Hell's Kitchen

Hendrix, Dante and Ferno called themselve's "215" because they were brothers from Jamaica. Hendrix was number "1" first born. Dante was "2" second oldest and Ferno was "5" the last born. This from the book Leviticus 2.15 (Bible) They also had "Locks", because of their faith. "Rastafari"

Int- 77th st Lexington Avenue, Ana with Tanya
walking toward the Six train Station

Ana- don't worry it looks worse than it is

Tanya- Damn I can't believe your Super doesn't mop up vomit in
the staircase, I bet you wasn't the only one who slipped on that
shit, you should see if you could sue for money

Ana- he's Dominican, you know how lazy those Dum-In-A-Cans
are, and we know he's broke

Tanya- (laughs then suddenly remember's in shock) Ay'dios
mijos, how're we going to raise the rest of the money for the
senior yearbooks?   ←

Ana- COIN'YO I totally forgot about those (Ana stops under a
dark brown canopy, as drizzle of rain begins sprinkling down,
waiting for street light change) I don't know, but we better
figure something out, cause the money has to get to Rosebaum
before Easter

Tanya- you know when my aunt went here like in the
seventy's she said that when they needed cash and couldn't
borrow enough money from the stores, they would put on a
show and have people pay to get in

Ana- A show?

Tanya- yeah, like singing and dancin'n'stuff

Ana- (laughing) who would come see these kids do anything,
nobody really has any talent and who'd pay money for it?

Tanya- parents, family, friends. Get like twentyfive people in a
show, and each one have four people come with them, that adds up
mami

Ana- but who would put the show together? You know we can't.

Tanya- my aunt said Mr. Bridge put on a show when she was
going here that blew up the spot

Ana- Mr.Bridge

Tanya- Uh huh, she told me people were dancing, singing, and alot
of people showed up jus from being family

Ana- (smiling) sounds like money

Tanya- and that chinito Nelson (reluctantly speaking) even though I think he a mad nerd, I heard he can dance his culo off
Ana- He's not a nerd Tanya
Tanya- whatever…well anyway you wanna go see Mr. Bridge tomorrow
Ana- he's not a nerd

        Camera pans away from Tanya kissing
        Ana on her cheek

        Ana crosses over to the downtown side of the six
        train, heading down subway steps out of view

                ~Scene end

          *   *

@ }—'--,-------------- 5

IT'S JUST A MOVIE KID

Int- A soul food Thanksgiving is being prepared in Seph's apartment. The classic Jazz Standard "A_train" is on vinyl in the background, as entrée's of everything from collards to hamhocks, is being dished out Sheila's kitchen.

Sheila walks over to the living room and lays the last pot of candied yams next to many trays of side dishes, surrounding a juicy turkey

Sheila- This food ain't gonna eat itself (taking off her mittens) COME AND GET IT

Everyone laughs and salutes happyThanksgiving, hugging and grabbing plates in line to fix a meal.

Ayqwom- Yo'Sef! Get those plastic ones out the kitchen these cups are too small
Seph- We don't have them cups no'more
Ayqwom- WHAT you mean we don't got THEM cups N'more, speakEnglish
Seph- You and Wraith used all THEM cups, THEM THEM, uncleTOMTOM
Sheila- Hey, hey, hey, don't you see we have visitors (jerking her head to Caucasians)
Ayqwom- Mom can you tell Seph to get more plastic cups from the Red Apple
Sheila- go get more cups Seph
Seph- (angry) I don't know why Qwam can't get them

A man well over six feet grabs Ayqwom

Jax- Cause Qwom and his pasty buddy

Ayqwom-Wraith daddy
Jax- (grinning) He and Wraith carried a fiftypound bird from WesternBeef this morn'n
Seph- (being handed money) k daddy what color
Jax- you pick baby boy (palming his head sending him off)

Nelson runs beside Seph but is called back by Sheila

Sheila- Jax wants to talk to you
Nelson-me?
Sheila- is there another lil'chingy chong here
Nelson- (going over) ok

Jax scoots over on the sofa, giving Nelson a spot to sit

Jax- Nelson Mandela my main MAN! Happy Thanksgiving son from the rising sun
Nelson- HappyThanksgiving, (smiling) rising sun?
Jax- YEAH Joe! That's where you from, don't you know it
Nelson- from the sun?
Jax- (new subject) I heard you're acting in a show at that theatre, next to the pig pen
Nelson- you mean the police station
Jax-same difference
Nelson- how'd ya find out?
Jax- I know James (Nelson looks up) and from what I heard you got some glide in that slide too
Nelson- I'm alright, Seph can dance
Jax- thanks but let's be real, I got two Black sons and both don't have one good foot put together (coughs) *doesn't help one wants to be pale rider*, but that's jus the breaks wit'kids (pause) you don't know what talent god gets at. (lighting a cigarette) But my boy sure fast on football
Nelson- Seph's real fast (excited) I see him run past every body!
Jax- (ignoring this) right, right, (blowing smoke) heard you was fighting for the Greys between classes

74

Speechless

Nelson- what?

Jax- my son keeps no secrets (grabs a bottle) at least from daddy

Nelson- I had no choice they run the school

Jax- don't have to apologize to me, in fact I hope you laid out some mayonnaise monkee's

Nelson- wush I could've'voided it, but fighting finds me wherever I hide

Jax- Nelson your Asian in New York, you're like a lightning rod for fights

Nelson- what you mean?

Jax- all the guys that aren't *you* feel that you're the bottom of the ladder when it comes to getting girls or anything MANLY so losing to you means they're the ultimate pussies

Nelson- serious

Jax- as cancer, that's why in your case I'm going to compliment you for punching a couple whiteboys in the face, cause although fighting in any sense is bad, but for your sake I'll give you a pass for trying to break that mold, and we all have a mold just in different ways

Nelson-thanks, I guess

Jax- remember one thing, if you do fight, *do it*, and do it GOOD. Don't jus knock'em on the ground and say yeah I floored him, FUCK HIM UP, specially the face , this way next time he plays bitch' wit a bunch of Chinese-Japanese whatever, he'll know how to act, he'll remember his cracked eyes and missing teeth

 SILENCE

Jax- (breaks the tension by changing subjects) why do you like dancing?

Nelson- guess I want to, that's all

Jax- and you're that good for people to parade your name about town jus cuz you want to? (Nelson goes speechless again) let me tell you sum'n nephew, it's not that you WANT to, it's that you NEED to release IT

Nelson- it makes me happy I guess

Jax- (puts out smoke) Nelson my Asian (closes rum bottle) sensation we need to get to the bottom of something (grins)

Nelson- (silent)

Jax- my son told me that you were interested in going to a school for this, is that right

Nelson- I haven't really thought about it

Jax- well incase you do, there some things you might need to know before diving into a world you know lil'bout

Nelson- I know a fella like me the odds would be uphill

Jax- would you know the way you look might put someone with a great deal of talent such as yourself at disadvantage?

Nelson- well I am short

Jax- you ain't that young now, and I know you got a mind, so stop playing possum. (smiles) cuz you ain't fool'n me. (grabs a plate from his wife kissing her, then putting it on the side)

Sheila- don't let that bird get cold daddy

Jax- thanks baby, I won't (sipping an iced glass of Captain Morgan, patting Sheila on the bum as she goes back to mind the guests) as you grow older people will constantly tell you how the world is complicated (pause) oh so complicated. But in fact the truth of the matter is, the world is too simple and animal

Nelson- Animal?

Jax- Very animal...And afraid of the unknown (smiles at Nelson) and you my round faced boy *is* the unknown.

Nelson- I'm not a big guy or bully, never was

Jax- no, but the bullys and big guys are afraid of you

Nelson- I don't get it

Jax- You're not as harmless as you think, and your energy is DEFINITELY a problem to selfish and weak people

Nelson-Weak people?

Jax- weak people do evil things Nelson, soon you will know this, in the films the plays you'll see, when you grow up

Nelson- I like the competition and when I feel it! BRICKS couldn't stop me SON, I mean Jax, sir

Jax- oh they won't come with BRICKS, they'll come with TV shows and music and movies

Nelson- that's all, just movies

Jax- yea but people are fooled by those movies Nelson (takes another sip of rum) you know I used to beatup and make fun of every Asian I ran into when I was a young'en

Nelson-(speechless)

Jax- I was fooled, and believed the hype and you will fall for the hype if theirs no education to teach you less

Nelson- Less, like low or different

Jax- you're not different, I just woke up one day and realized making fun of ya'll is like laughing at myself (finishes drink, loud tap on glass) cause I'm at the other end, see they have me as a GOON, a no-brain goblin and that means no MONEY and after the good times with the white woman they leave for higher ground (lifts a box of stogies) but for you, anybody can whup yo ass, all races beat you, as Whitee's concerned

Nelson- Guess that's why my dad calls me "Last place shit son of bitch in America"

Jax- well you sure roughed up my son the first day we moved here from the Bronx.

Nelson- sorry Jax

Jax- For what, you untaught my son alot of bad things I taught him. You might not know this, but if not seeing my own seed getting pummeled by the enemy I may never have awoken. When you beat my son's ass, believe it or not I was actually joyful in my heart.

Nelson- Joy to see your son hurt

Jax- No. Joyful to see that a real man can exist outside one race, and that simply we live in a country run by them so how could I have never realized that the real man is going to be HIM, whether true, or FALSE

Nelson-Jax I don't know, I'm confused

Jax- (a match is struck and the flame illuminates a fiery red upon Jax's face, lighting up the old cigarette again) I see your confusion, but believe you me, knowing theres a kid on your side kick'n ass in all manner of ways you're not supposed'n this part of the world, makes me have life that there's a Blackman in these parts AS WELL that has a beautiful mind, and is a real man (blows smoke in Nelson's face) jus like you

Nelson- Seph can beat me up now, he outgrew me

Jax- Nelson your fight doesn't come like that. When I came back home after six'nine (Medal of Honor twinkling on glass table) I lost all faith in God, or faith of ANY KIND, war effects people like that, it was not chance I saw you kick my sons ass, punch out the other racist kid my son was hang'n wit', mr. white Dragon. All who outsized and weighed you by plenty. I realized there must be something (looks beyond Nelson's head with wild eyes) trying to TOUCH US from the otherside

Nelson- you think I'm possessed by the devil

Jax- (laughs) no, not at all (closes eyes while speaking) but if you w*uzz*... do you think it always the devil who scratches you (puts his cigarette out in his palm, eyes opening) or could it be something else

Nelson- you mean like Jesus

Jax- ANYTHING, just something intent on bringing balance after all that's what nature does best (grins deeply) *isn't it*

Nelson- I don't want to sound greedy but I'm not trying to make other Asian guys feel good, it makes ME feel good and I love performing in a way that can't be, you know...

Jax- well that's good, because that's exactly the kind'a heart it's going to take *when* you win Oscar

Nelson-When?

Jax- Yeah, when you win your first Academy award, and the first as the last thing they want to see

A platinum moment of silence

Sheila- JAX! You still haven't touched your plate!

Strange air which loomed about Nelson and Jax disappear only a slight tingle remains, till all is forgotten as it never was

78

Jax- oh I'm sorry baby, me and my Golden child apprentice here was just talking business

Sheila- (scoffing) Oh please' what kind of business this little ching-chong fucker know, he just as short as his daddy

Jax- Did my son come back wit the cups?

Seph- Right here daddy! (Snow covered jacket)

Ayqwom- who the fuck picks PINK? You're a punk you know that!

Sheila- you got snow all over the colla' greens SEPH! Get that damn jacket into the bathroom (shrieking) YU-SEPH!!

Nelson-thanks Jax

Jax- Just get me some good seats when you stroll down that red carpet (winks)

Nelson- k

_End Scene

   6

WHY DON'T YOU TRY OUT LES'GUARDANTS?

Int- Ehmet Ray's "I'll see you in my dreams" fills the background, as shots of different aspects of the holiday season collage into frames, shot after shot

Clip 1- Lamott and Taheem in the back of Ms. Kietz's science class with Santa hats on watching Ana walk toward them, making her way to her seat

Ana- excuse me (softly)
Taheem- WHAT?
Ana- my seat (looking at the desk to his right)
Taheem-WELL!!!… (StoneFaced)

Lamott gets up taking off Santa hat

Taheem- (doing the same with warm smile) why didn't you say so
Ana-(daunted) uh…thanks
Taheem-happy holidays

Clip 2- Shots of a New York winters' night, very clear, and crisp

Shot 1- 23rd st and 10th ave, group of women in construction and Fireman gear having snowball fight with another group of men dressed in womens wigs, skirts and high heels (drag)
Shot 2- Greyhound bus driving by with giant poster of Maculey Culkin's face clasped between his hands "Home Alone"
Shot-3- At 315 Bowery street can be heard sounds of glass breaking, and scents of pot being smoked by six pale white teens with Bald heads, decked out Black MA1's and knee high Doc Martin boots, smoking outside CBGB's. Each military flyer emblemed with three letters "DMS"
Shot 4-Alec walking into Southerly pharmacy with empty bookbag and VHS tape

Shot 5- Alec with Steinbeck shaking his head in disbelief as Alec slaps the tape and says "I made copies so if you feel like snatching this up, you're going to be in RIKERS Isle before breakfast SHORTEYES" (Steinbeck~p.68) a moment later Steinbeck goes to all the cashiers "This kid is my son from my first wife... Anything he walks out with is under the table" then gives Al a basket and shakes his hand, after which he leaves abruptly, up the aisle, ramming into a worker stocking the shelves, knocking down all kinds of CREATINE BUCKETS

Clip 3- Tanya talking to Mr. Bridge

Mr. Bridge- I haven't done a show in over ten year's
Tanya- Please Mr.B we can't collect enough money for the yearbooks!
Mr. Bridge- did you ask all the pizza shops and bagel places around here (smirking) god knows they make a fortune off these children at Ox
Tanya- (Impatiently) we asked all them and it's still not enough!
Mr. Bridge- easy, easy, I'll talk to principal Rosebaum (soothing her) then I'll get back to you
Tanya- Oh I knew you'd come THRU
Mr. Bridge- I'm only asking, there's no promises
Tanya- (rushing away) thanks for doing it Mr. B, thanks so much!

Ehmet Ray's strings fade out

Clip 4- Joel the doorman and Seph are doing a rendition of Run DMC's "Christmas Carol"

Seph has a bright blue sweater that says "It's Christmas BEE-YOTCH!!" and Joe is wearing fake antlers with bells at the lobby. The radio is blasting

Joel- It was December twentyfourth on Hollis ave in the dark when I see a man chilling with his dog in the park- I approached very slowly with my heart full of fear- looked at his dog, oh my god an ill reindeer!- but then I was illin cause the man had a beard, and a bag full of goodies twelve o'clock had neared- so I turned my head a second and the man had gone- but he left his driver's wallet smacked dead on the lawn- I picked the wallet up then took a pause- took out the license and it cold said Santa Clause- a million dollars in it, cold hundreds of G's, enough to buy a boat and matching car with ease- but I'd never steal from santa, cause that ain't right- so I went home to mail it back to him that same night- but when I got home, I bugged, cause under the tree- was a letter from Santa and all the DOUGH WAS FOR ME!

The beat goes on and they both do a silly dance together till Seph's part comes on

Seph- It's Christmas time, in Hollis Queens- moms cook'n chicken and collard greens- rice and stuffing, macaroni and cheese- and Santa put gifts under Christmas tree's- decorate the house with lights at night- snow's on the ground, snow white so bright- in the fireplace is the yule log- beneath the mistle toe as we drink eggnog- the rhymes you hear are the rhymes of Daryl's- but each and every year we bust Christmas carols

The beat goes into a Christmas melody and they do the silly dance as tenants are now entering

Seph and Joel- Rhymes so loud and proud you hear it- it's Christmas time and we got the spirit- jack frost chillin, the orch is out- and that's what Christmas is all about- the time is now, the place is here- and the whole wide world is filled with cheer

Seph- my name's D.M.C with the mic in my hand- and I'm chillin and coolin just like the Snowman- so open your eyes, lend us an ear

Seph and Joel- WE WANT TO SAY MERRY CHRISTMAS AND HAPPY NEW YEAR!!

They both hug and give pounds till the song goes out the radio, suddenly Frank the superintendent comes in

Frank- fuck kind'a songs that?
Seph- come on Frank it's the holidays
Frank- yeah, holidays, so play some Bing Crosby or Nat King Cole not this junky music
Joel- (laughing) Junky music? This is the shit they play in the Bronx
Frank- Then play when you go up! (turns radio off) anyway (hands Joel an envelope which Joel opens right away) merry Christmas
Joel-YES! (lifting twenty dollar bills) Thanks frank, Merry Christmas to you too
Seph- (leaning on Frank) hey
Frank- HEY what?
Seph- where's my gift
Frank- up your ass-COLO if you don't get off ME!
Seph-(runs out) UP your ass-COLO, Frankie-GRINCH!

Clip 5- Ana is wrapping gifts with her mother Emily

Bobo- fifteen minutes till your sweetheart jumps on stage wit his thong
Emily- dear Allah, hurry kids
Ana- HERE! (throwing Bobo a wrapped present) put that under
Bobo- Under what!
Ana- The tree! Pentheho! (grabbing her coat)
Bobo- I hate this time of year
Emily- (putting on her jacket) Gordo! Bring the camera from the kitchen!
Ana- you ready ?
Emily- (hand on her shoulder) come on mela', lets go

Clip 6- Nelson speaks to a tall army clad man on stage

Jack- You know when they get here you'll have to hide

Hiro- (almost naked) YES, hi-DU... I know
Jack- (grinning) Did you like the chocolates?
Hiro- (Japanese mix with English) chokoreto te nan'desuka?
(confused)
Jack- (showing wrapper of Hershey Bar) you know, Cho-co-latt
Hiro- (excitedly) YES! Yes I loff CHO-KO-LAT!
Jack- (laughing) goodboy, goodboy, you know you remind me of
my kid back home (taking out a black and white photo handing it
to Nelson) you're not much older then he is and he loves
Hershey's just as much "he's a bit taller" but your tough so its ok
Hiro- Hershy nani desu?
Jack- you know Cho- co- latt
Hiro- OH! (pointing at wrapper) Ita chokoreto hershey'desu
(wide eyed) AH, I KNOW I KNOW!
Jack- (laughing) you know you're a real lightbulb kid?
Hiro-Li-too-BUL?
Jack- yeah... (suddenly a sound of splitting branch echoes through
the stage, making the man snap up his rifle and point to the sound)
WHO'S THERE? (Nelson hides under a make shift bush few feet
from the mans boot)

       Ana can be seen with Bobo next to her watching intensely
with the rest of the audience

       End of play
       ~There's a PT-109 boat next to a painting of a river on
  stage

Tom- Did you tell Billy about them hookers we banged on
Sai'Pan
Jack- No, why?
Tom- (looking devilish) Good' cause it's an inside thing

Jack- Nothing the MP's have to worry about right?

Tom- no (shoving him toward picture of boat) and nothing
you have to worry bout' either JACK!
Jack-WASH your PRICK (Tom laughing on Jack's shoulder,
followed by a slight sigh) I'm sure gonna miss this little island

Tom- easy for you to say, I still gotta run down these JAP nutzo's in these cur-Zed hills (looking up at painting of a mountain) somebody didn't tell these Bozo's the wars over...

Nelson jumps out a makeshift tree with a rifle bigger then himself and points at Tom

Jack-HIRO!
Tom- (pulling out his side pistol) Jack get down!
Jack- (running toward Tom) Tom no! (wrestling the gun out his hand)
Hiro-KUMA!

Clap of firearm, smoke floods the stage

Jack falls onto Tom's side

Hiro- (dropping rifle, running over to Jack) Jac-KU! Jac-KU!
Tom- (looking stunned at Jack who is dying in his arms laying him down) why did you...
Jack- Tom I should'a told you (holding his chest on the ground) hiro (gasping) come here boy (waving gently) I want you to have this
Tom- this kid shot you, who is this? (screaming toward picture of boat) BILLY! BILLY! (A man comes out backstage, where the PT-109 is drawn)
Billy- where's the fire! Can't you see I'm egg and bacon busy... (see's Jack shot) HOLY JESUS, MARY AND JOSEPH!
Tom- Get the goddamn first aid kit NOW!
Jack- (handing Nelson a necklace with an emblem that he rips off his neck) Do you know what this is kid
Hiro- (shaking his head holding the cross and symbol) NO, NO! (handing it back)
Jack- Listen KID! (shoving it in his palm) this here's Saint Jude, patron saint of lost causes (bombs can be heard thundering in the distance) heaven knows you're gonna need it

Tom- Jack you crazy leatherneck, what'd I tell you bout that big heart of yours
Jack- stick a cork in it Tommy, this here's my son (winking at Nelson) and don't ever let'm tell ya'different
Hiro-(sobbing) Wasurenaiyo
Billy- (running on spot with medical kit) where's he hit? (kneeling down to work on him)
Jack- Billy? Did you know Tom here laid down some pipe on Sai'Pan? (shell of his voice)
Billy- no (out of it) no I didn't Jack
Jack- Guess he owe's you some nucky'poonTANG
Billy- your gonna have to keep your head up pal
Tom- (picking up the young boys rifle) Jack? (whispering) this...this is your gun

      Jack passes in Hiro's arms, still slightly laughing from his own dying last words "nucky'poonTANG"

      Lights close, as everyone gets up to cheer. Ana is crying and so is Bobo

                        ~Scene fades

      Int- Ana walks out theater holding Nelson's hand, through crowd of people mostly smoking

Nelson- hope your booty isn't too sore
Ana- are you crazy, loved it !

      Camera follows them. The angle shot is side viewed, past Ana's face into the street, where cars are passing.
      "Perfect combination" by Stacy Latisaw begins to chime in

Ana- Ever thought about going to Les'Guardant's (eye's sparkling in cold night)
Nelson- I don't know (sighing) this is jus'off Broadway stuff (opening door to Blimpies, ladies first) anyway I didn't audition

for this (saying hi to Maria the manager) this guy Jim just begged me to do it, so I did him a favor

Ana- Jim, that short old scruffy look'n guy? He begged you?

Nelson- (laughing) scruffy looking' (takes her coat and hangs it behind the booth) it's not what you think, they needed a young Asian boy, and I jus happen to be it

Ana- so you must be good then if you don't even have to try

Nelson- Ana (grinning) I just got lucky (looking as if he doesn't want to continue) Two hot chocolate's maria

Ana- Maria! (calling her back) make that one hot chocolate

Nelson- you don't want nutth'n?

Ana- no, I want some hot cocoa, its jus I don't want alot (glowing) can I take few sips of yours

Maria- *Mira su culo que grande!*

Ana- (laughing) *si mami*

Nelson- ok, whats the deal (looking at both of them) you guys making fun of me

Maria- here (handing him a hot cup of cocoa) you don't have to pay

Nelson- you sure ?

Maria- don't worry I charge you double next time

Ana- (laughing) thank you (pulling Nelson to the window seat)

Nelson- so was I the butt of another joke?

Ana- no but we was joking about your butt

Nelson- oh shut up (kicking her under the table)

Ana- damn, why you gotta be so rough (taking a sip, sliding it to Nelson) be careful papi, it's very hot

Nelson- (burning his lips) Oww, that is Hot!

Ana- (laughing) so innocent

Nelson- I'm not innocent

Ana- yes you are

Nelson- no I'm not!

Ana- you look like a baby in that play, with your thong and no clothes

Nelson- oh man, you gonna tell everybody I was butt naked tomorrow

Ana- no I'm not (suddenly serious, stirring the cup with coffee stir) I don't want anyone to know what I saw you in (very quiet, looking at cocoa)
Nelson-(Grabs her hand) Ana...what's wrong?
Ana-(looks up never blinking) I think, sometimes... (A tear falls) why' you never ask me out...
Nelson-(deep stare, whispers) come here

They finally kiss with snow falling outside the window and a steaming cup smoking between them

Blimpies huge windows fog up from inside.
*StacyLatisaw's voice fades

After a moment nothing but mist can be seen on the glass. It stays this way for a beat, then unfogs itself with Seph coming out a vaporized bathroom, concluding his shower

Radio is on forecast of weather, as Seph dresses next to an "Al-B'Sure" poster and steps out the house

Radio- Hope you New Yorker's have your rubber galoshes and Tote's umbrella's this weekend, cause there's going to be a Blast of early Christmas blizzard coming our way, morning or even as quick as tonight, with temperatures dropping to single digits and windchill advisory's down to fifteen to twenty below, more on the... (Out the door)

Seph steps off the elevator and see's Alec waiting for him at the lobby

Alec- free at "Sound Factory" tonight
Seph- did you tell Nel
Alec- Nah man, I haven't seen that dude all week
Seph- I ran into Moses'P last night and he told me Ann and him were sitt'n at Blimpie's kiss'n
Alec- no way

Seph- dead ass, said it went on for good minute too
Alec- Ain't Paul doin candid camera
Seph- like you can talk
Alec- Fuck you
Seph- heard them Air Force nigga's be runnin the Factory
Alec- Yeah but Cack and Turk is gonna be there wit TNT
Seph- you think they let you dance wit them if they battle
Alec- I got some steps that I made up off Nelson's move into some new shit
Seph- no you don't nigga (sucking his teeth)
Alec- (ignoring) If they battle I'm gon' help them take ova' that spot
Seph- (amused) uh, right
Alec- you'll see

    The scene changes to night, where outside Sound Factory many of the club goers are obviously not dressed for the elements

    Seph watches Alec get out cab running toward him

Alec- Did you see Nelson?
Seph- Nah, did you?
Alec- what you think I asked you for
Seph- left a message on his answering machine, happy
Alec-Think he gon' show
Seph- I don't know but Turk jus went in and I think Cactus and Stretch is already in there
Alec- well (undecided)
Seph- what?
Alec- well let's see what happens
Seph- you gon' dance wit them
Alec- I don't know

    A gay Hispanic male opens the velvet rope and taps Alec

Picker- how many

Alec- (looking up the block again)

Picker- you look good Mulatto, but not Ignore'me'good (shifts his weight) how many?

Alec- (not paying attention) Hold on

Seph- Al! He asked you a question!

Alec- (reluctantly) SHIT ain't showed!

Picker- SHITTY'SHITTY GANG'BANG, HOW MANY HARRY BELLA'FON'TAY

Alec- I mean two, jus me and him

Picker- (taps Alec again) MR. LARUSSO

Alec- what?

Picker- the lounge in the club is very dark, if it get too dim, just light 'up them candles' in your EARHOLEMUTHAFUCKA!

       Alec and Seph walk in and immediately feel the bass (Jungle Brothers "Girl I"ll house you" is pumping)

Seph- Damn, I haven't heard the lowend like this since "Red Zone"

       Seph see's a huge circle beginning to expand near the center of the dance floor, as he and Alec walk down a ramp leading toward the battle

Alec- come on, them nigga's is already started

Seph-they look outnumbered

       The views of the club will be shot in compilation of angles

View 1- Top angle looking down on Dj and two spinning record's, that his fingertips are guiding back and forth from the fader

View 2- close up of blue light spinning through the backdrop of a mirror. *Contrast confirms the deep darkness of the walls inside SoundFactory

View 3- sideview of dancing couples, being pushed back by
a circle of battle that's exploding out

View 4- Dj spins record and cuts to part of the song where
there's an alarm "TOOBLACK...TOOSTRONG"

View 5- Instantly a shot of four individuals from top to bottom
army gear down, standing in the middle of the dancefloor with
their heads bowed

View 6- Turk, Cactus, and Stretch are standing opposite them

They seem to be silent until Seph and Alec come over

Alec- yo'yo'yo, what up T-Bone
Turk- (strictly business) is Nelson here?
Alec- nah, we didn't see him
Cactus- (two more army fatigued figures add on to the four
already standing) THREE'six
Turk- is he cumm'n?
Alec- I don't know, why?
Turk- (one of the army clad members steps out line) nothing,
forget it (Turk turns away from Al, walks to the end of his
crew, then begins to tighten his shoes)
Cactus- is that Japanese kid here?
Turk-nah
Stretch- FUCK! (staring hard at Air Force One) I hate them
nigga's

"Video Crash" by Tyree Storms out the speakers

The battle begins with a Boom of Bass, as the
first move is made by the littlest one wearing army gear

The battle ends with Turk, Cactus, Stretch, and Alec leaving the club in shame, outnumbered during the showdown they quickly turn the missing member as the goat

Cactus- how the choosers let all those Air Force bitches in with no girls
Turk- cock suckers
Cactus- (looking at Alec) why that Chinese kid didn't show up
Alec- you mean Nelson?
Cactus- Whateva, why he not come
Alex- (confused) I don't know
Turk- (now out the club all of them, Turk hails a cab) tell that poser next time you see him, not to appear in any of the sessions
Alec- ah, come on T, he prolly didn't have any money to get in
Seph-free night remember
Turk- I don't give a FUCK (slams door of cab driving off in mad dash)

Seph and Alec are left stranded far from home

Seph- (slipping on ice covered girder) yo, X'
Alec- what
Seph-how much money you got
Alec- dollar
Seph- shit NEGRO that all you got
Alec- yeah 'why
Seph- we on twelve HERB ... as in Twelth AVE
Alec-so
Seph- its five long avenues to the subway and thru Chelsea projects
Alec- you don't have money for cab?
Seph- NO
Alec- Fuck
Seph- told yo ass not to buy apples for them
Alec-they need energy to throwdown, you don't know you ain't a dancer

93

Seph- Man stop ride'n them nigga's jockstrap! Everytime you brought them an apple they threw them shits at ya'head
Alec- whateva
Seph- yeah, whateva the fuck whateava, how the fuck we gon'get home
Alec- you seen "Temple of Doom" (chucks granny smith at a snow plow grinding by) WE WALK, FROM HERE!

They head uptown (beside the Hudson River) hands in jacket pockets, as the winter storm deposits white all around them, as they trudge through the snow packed concrete

~Scene End

@ }—'--,--------------- 7

WHERE'S THE AUDITION?

Int- Nelson waking up in bed, his room is icyblue, lighted quietness to the coming snow

Telephone rings

Nelson- (half asleep) hello… Cris, time is it… Classes're off (pause) nah I gotta go to school (pause) lucky bastard… what you mean... shoot, forty dollar's a car, whoa… I'd love too but don't have a shovel… alright then, it's been a while since I cut, but… sounds like it be worth it, where we doin this…Gracie Mansion… cool see you there (hangs up)

~Scene fades

Int- Ana sitting with Taheem and Craig beside her in homeroom

Craig- Yo Ana, (headphones on, blasting"Poison" by B.B.D) you got any sisters
Taheem-Or cousins
Ana- why?

Lamott walks by and sits on her otherside

Lamott- You do know *fine brotha's* is available
Ana- Yea'right! You probably rape them
Lamott- WHO ME (wolfish) never
Taheem- you mean they try to rape me banana (smoothly) right Ana
Ana- oh sure Taheem, they all want you

Darcy passes infront of the four and gives them a dirty look, especially Ana.

Craig picks up on it

Craig- (singing from his walkman) "That girl is poison, never trust a big butt and a smile"
Ana- she look dirty
Lamott- I'd let her suck myDICK' tho
Ana- Lamott please, you'd let anything with two pink lips go down on you
Lamott- or purple
Taheem- (serious) why that girl always be hawk'n you
Ana- I don't know
Taheem- (pause) so my little man nel play'n both y'all like a cat on a string, huh?
Ana- shut up Ta-HEEM
Lamott- uh oh Tah, I think you touched a nerve
Craig- he must make really good eggrolls to have Italian chicks and Puerto Rican girls' fight'n ova him
Ana- I usually fight under him (winks, as the whole crew OH's and Taheem smiles)

School intercom

Message- Hello, this is Mr. Bridge of English lit. Student Government is planning a show for Spring, to help budget some of the funds unable to cover end of year fees. We are asking anyone with desire and passion for self expression to come to the audition, which will be held afterschool this evening, at the auditorium. Only eighth graders and seniors will be allowed to audition, please note that those who will be selected will most likely have to stay well into evening hours, so if your parents will not allow you to come home late, please do not come to tryouts this afternoon, thank you (buzz tone ends the announcement)

Ana- (shocked, whispering) they did it
Taheem-did what?
Ana- nothing (getting up walking out)

She runs into the hall and runs right into

Tanya- Can you believe it!
Ana- This is so crazy! We came with this
Tanya- I came up wit it mami
Ana- Ms. Smarty pants
Tanya- bet your Nelson's gonna make it easy
Ana- (Stunned) He didn't come to homeroom
Tanya- he's probably late again, you know that chinito always miss homeroom
Ana- yeah, but he's been early all week
Tanya- Relax mami! You're not married to him or anything
Ana- (trying to hide emotion) That Russian kid has him in his last period
Tanya- who Ermin? (Glances at Hermin)
Ana- that's his name (Tanya nods, as Ana walks over) excuse me
Hermin-(smiling) hi
Ana- is Nelson in Sapt's class wit you last period
Hermin- I believe he is young lady
Tanya- (attitude) just let us know if you see the PRICK
Hermin- If I see NELSON! I'll let you fine ladies know (nicely to Ana) well, jus you princess'Di (curtly to Tanya) good day miss
Ana- (being pulled away by Tanya) wow, nelson has cute friends
Tanya- oh pleeze, you saw his teeth and big hairy hands
Ana- (sexy tone) I like BIG hands
Tanya- oh shut up puta
Ana- (laughing, sucking her teeth) you're a puta, PUTA

~Sceneend

Int- Custodial engineer is seen mopping the third floor, a second later a period bell rings and children swarm the hallway. The view blurs in and out where he appears on the second floor, throwing out garbage as kids run around with fake bones and flowers past the janitor emptying the litter bin. The final bell rings and he sweeps clean the front entrance where he stops and rests. Janitor wipes his brow of sweat and disappears after muttering few words in Scottish accent "DEITHT'BYRTTH"

Reah walks into homeroom

Reah- Anne
Ana- yes
Reah- Nelson didn't show up to world history, Erm told me to tell you (she leaves)
Ana- k, thanks

Tanya walks over to her

Ana- he didn't show all day (nervous)
Tanya- sorry'dee
Ana- Damn! I really wanted him to be in it (frustrated) he's so good at it

Ana kicks a chair, clanking it loudly off the desk

Ms. Pembell- ladies I'm afraid you're going to have to continue this conversation outside (Ana and Tanya are in homeroom, where Ms. Pembell is coat and bag ready to leave)
Tanya- come on mami, we better go (Ana remains silent)

Walking past the security table, Ana peaks inside the auditorium before heading out. She sees more then forty kids inside taking off their bags and coats placing them on fold seats

Tanya- maybe you could ask Mr. Bridge for a favor or something, he seems to like you

Ana- you know if he put Nelson in after all them kids had to fight for thier spots he's going to lose respect from the whole school!

They walk out silent and uncomfortable, when all of a sudden Bobo runs right into Tanya panting for breath

Tanya- What the FUCK man!

Bobo- (mocking her) *what the fuck man*
Ana- don't play
Tanya- Were you cutting again Gordo
Bobo- NO
Ana- then why were you coming from the otherside of the block

Bobo- I got out halfday cause our trip got cancelled stupid (looking up) damn why you two so bitchy
Ana- shut up nobody's being bitchy, stinky
Tanya- Mr. Bridge is throwing an audition for a show and Nelson didn't show up
Bobo- I jus saw him
Ana- (booming) WHAT
Bobo- yea, he was with that white kid
Ana-Cris?
Bobo- yea, and they were (laughing over what he saw) shoveling the street
Tanya- shoveling the street?
Ana- (overriding everything) WHERE
Tanya- what the hells' he doing shoveling the street?
Bobo- I don't know, maybe he got caught hoppin'da'train, why you asking me
Ana- Forget that! WHERE STUPID! (twisting his ear)
Bobo- up on eighty'ninth (in pain)
Ana- What ave?
Bobo- second I think (finally free) DAMN bitch, you crazy!
Tanya-that'sfar
Ana- (hurriedly) Tanya how much money you have
Tanya-what?

Ana- no time to explain, jus tell me
Tanya- fifty cents why?
Ana- Ungh! (pushes her brother) how much you got
Bobo- why (knowing what's next face)
Ana-ok, give it to me gordo
Bobo- what the fuck
Ana- if you don't I'll tell mama
Bobo- tell mama what
Ana- tell mommy you cut today
Bobo- FUCK, I need that for my brisket of beef! I'm hungry, I missed lunch
Tanya- Gordo give her the money, you can survive on that fat for weeks (grabs a handful of fat on Bobo's stomach) months I mean
Bobo- (slapping her hand) fuck off bitch
Ana- Money Ding'Dong, NOW!
Bobo- (handing her a few bills, watching her count) I hate that fuck'n chino, even by accident he ruins my day
Ana- there's only four dollars here
Tanya- that'll be enough for you to take a cab there
Ana- I'm gonna take the train then ride the taxi back together (she runs off, dropping her bookbag)
Tanya- go mami, GO!
Bobo- (picking up her bag) I should pee on this

     Camera pans on Ana running up Lexington, then turns into Sal's pizza across the street, over the heads of students shuffling in, where a clock on the wall displays three fifteen 3:15

     Blurring out of sight, then back into focus it now reads three fortynine 3:49 with the sound of a cab screeching in front of the junior high school

Ana-GO-GO-GO (pushing Nelson out cab)
Nelson- I don't know if I want to do this
Ana- (slamming cab door) SURE YOU DO (dragging Nelson into Oxford with her)

They both stand in front of auditorium doors

Guard 1- you know they didn't start yet right
Ana- they didn't?
Guard 2- Nope
Nelson- thought you said we were late (turning to Ana)
Guard 1- you would've been if the stage wasn't wet from the
snow that melted through da'ruf Saturday
Ana- (captures a moment) Nelson
Nelson- yes
Ana- (kisses him on cheek, then looks softly up) go in

Nelson stalls

Guard 1- gotta lock the doors outfront, (holding keys) you in or
out
Nelson- Ana (slows his speech) do you want me away
Ana- I know how much you love it, yes
Nelson- (pecks Ana on the lips and dashes in) YOU KNOW
THERES NO GUARANTEE THAT I'M GONNA GET
MADE!
All the kids waiting in chairs snap their necks back to
see the commotion

Mr. Bridge- Nelson! Are you auditioning?
Nelson- yes, uh, I want to dance

The whole auditorium booms in laughter

Mr. Bridge- QUIET! (kids settle down) Well I suggest you
sit down and shut your hole like everyone else

Nelson ghostly sits down next to a girl strangely familiar
She looks at him for a second, then moves over few
seats next to two of her friends. Ana looks down and smiles, then
glints a slight shimmer from Mr. Bridge beaming at her

Guard 2- You're going to have to move from there
Ana- (catches one last glance, as the music starts to play, then turns to head out) thanks
Guard 1- for what (Ana walks out, door closing behind her slowly)
Guard 1- (making sure door is securely shut) these kids is getting stranger and stranger, I tell'ya Joyce
Guard 2- Yeah, and doin' the nasty much younger too
Guard1-Eh'Humm (approvingly)

Camera overlooks the stage where Bridge's back is seen and faces of the students are all on him, reflecting light that is hitting off the glazed wood stage onto seats infront, leaving the rear chairs in utter darkness.

Mr. Bridge- ALL EYES ON ME! (Remote in hand, shutting off music) Out of all you who came, who here is really serious about performing on stage. (out the fifty or so sitting, few remain after all the hands are raised to sit with arms down)

Mr. Bridge- KEEP YOUR HANDS UP ALL OF YOU (he begins to walk towards the kids with hands lowered) excuse me are you deaf (to a redneck teen with baggy pants)
Kid hand down – (silence)
Mr. Bridge- I'm going to ask everyone sitting with their hands rested the same question. ARE YOU DEAF

In unison all the students sitting very coolly, slouched on their seats, hands lowered, do a collage of rude antics and smart remarks. Thee redneck one is still mute

After few moments of disrespect the teacher acts

Mr. Bridge- all of you not taking this seriously get up and meet me at security desk

Slowly all the sly ones which happen to be a dozen or so, start to trudge up the ramp inbetween seats out the doors of the auditorium. When all are out Mr. Bridge comes back alone, only to hear a shout out from Nadja

Guard 2- You want me to throw all'em out!
Mr. Bridge- Yes all, right out, thank you very much
Guard 1- What, they can't sing'dance
Mr. Bridge- They're a Rock band, called "THE REJECTS"
 (slams door)

Children are quiet

Mr. Bridge- Now, although only the good of heart remain, there will still be more leaving, but not on the account of being CINTUS' SUPREMUS

Nelson cackles, but no one is laughing

Mr. Bridge- Are you an asshole
Nelson- uh, no
Mr.Bridge- don't sound confident
Nelson- I'm not!
Mr. Bridge- is someone raising their voice (grinning deeply)
Nelson- no
Mr. Bridge- no what

The same girl Nelson thought looked familiar is staring strangely at him from down row. He notices but jus glances away and humbles himself

Nelson- no mister Bridge
Mr. Bridge- (now panning whole group) THINK WE'VE WASTED ENOUGH TIME DON'T YOU (looking at a light skin boy checking his pager)
Michael- yes sir, Mr. Bridge (puts it away)

The teacher walks up stage

Mr. Bridge- this (picks up device) is remote for the CD. When I press play music will begin. (He points toward the system located in corner, next to piano and three flags, American stars and stripes in the middle) NOW I WANT ALL OF YOU TO COME UP, Hurry now

The children trade places with the teacher. All students are now on stage and Mr. Bridge is down sitting in the center row looking up

Mr. Bridge- when music begins all of you are to dance in place (takes a moment) Sometime after the first song ends I will begin to tap people on their shoulder, those that feel my hand will have to sit

Crowd upstage is silenced at the final words :
Music begins

Mr.Bridge-DANCE!

All begin to move to the music, slowly at first, but then many pick up pace. "Work it to the Bone" by LNR is running through the speakers while students are grooving in place. Some stand out the crowd, while many are struggling to hold the rhythm. A few begin to trance out and really begin to let loose melodically with their bodies, Nelson spins on one hand in the air, than flips down tap dancing

The song ends, another begins "World Famous" by M. Mclaren is now playing and the beat of the song is much slower and smoother then the one that just went off. Two thirds of the children are now completely lost, but a boy named Abdul makes the transition almost naturally. Mr. Bridge is now making his way up and many begin to eye him

Mr. Bridge- Please continue till music ends, I do not recall telling anyone to stop

    Students are now dancing off'beat, nervous from watching Bridge step around them, jamming, as he makes the first touch of the audition

Danielle- I thought she was doing good (speaking of Kyoko who has just been tapped and is now walking off stage)
    Mr. Bridge turns to Danielle immediately and begins to walk over

Farooz- uh oh, don't look now but I think he heard you Danny
Danielle- shoot

    Danielle is tapped and makes her way off stage
    Nelson stares as she walks to her seat
    Suddenly a short black boy jumps in front of him

Abdul- Yo, what is you?
Nelson- (stunned, stopping movement) What?
Abdul- (dancing closer) You mixed?

    Nelson who is completely motionless feels two quick pats on his shoulder

Nelson- Damn! (upset) Why you talk to me for!? (Storming off)
Abdul-(laughing) Sit down CHOW'MAIN

    Abdul is immediately touched right after

    The audition ends with more then half the children who came to take part jumbled in their seats with jackets and bags. Sweat is on the faces of all still up

Mr. Bridge- (pointing remote to CD system turning off music) to all those sitting, I thank you all for coming and appreciate the effort you gave. (he turns to stage where children are drenched) To all the players still on stage you have so much spirit and heart. But for this production, rhythm is most important and I'm sure you'll find ways to help SGO in other fields. Thank you for giving all you got (he waves them down) grab your things, and Joyce at the desk will assist you out. Bless you and get home safe

A pair of girls bawl out in amazement

Raven-FUCK ME!
Bella- (Stunned as her friend) Yeah, uh, YOU KNOW!

Others are also baffled

Abdul-DANG`Yo!!
Nelson-what!
Abdul- you mixed?

From the otherside of Nelson's row, Danielle glances over

Danielle- Farooz, I seen that boy before
Farooz- Yeah, he's that Oriental hanging with the Blacks outside at lunch (turning bad mood) I saw him fighting a few weeks ago
Danielle- He was fighting? (unbelieving) Yea'RIGHT
Farooz- Okay, don't believe me but he's trouble, and his friends bully and scare the crap out of all the "SP" kids

Danielle focuses on Nelson as Bridge speaks

Mr. Bridge- Some of you might be wondering why you're still here (pause) And yes I'm talking 'bout the one's who have absolutely no dancing ability (pause) The reason is simple, yes the show is mostly body in motion, but there is star quality in appearance as well (looking at Bella) so I've permitted some of you to stay, but only in the strictest condition that you'll try your very best to learn the moves in the show. Lord knows some of you will have to go beyond rehearsals to pick up steps, so I've decided to pencil instructors from this bunch, to tutor slower kids

Bella- Oh no
Raven- what?
Bella- (touching up her make up) what you mean WHAT, I'm gonna'have to stay late and teach dance to the retards

A girl from the back row yells out

LaTanya- OH Please skinny white girl, nobody wants to learn nothing from you, end up look'n like a seizure attack, bitch!

Most of the auditorium breaks into laughter

Mr. Bridge- LATANYA! This is not the Bronx Zoo! (waits silently for attitude, then goes on) On the desk outside where the guards sit, there's a box with approval sheets to be signed by parent or guardian, these are to be brought back here tomorrow, any questions
Chantae- when is auditions, I mean rehearsals?
Mr. Bridge- All information will be on consent forms, I will announce names of tutors tomorrow evening and please bring sweats and extra socks, I don't want this auditorium funking up while I'm in here. (turns his back on students) good day

Most have left while a few as in Michael and Abdul are putting away things for Mr. Bridge

Michael- (breaking off from Abdul, runs to Nelson) Yo!
Nelson-sup?
Michael- where you learn to dance like that
Nelson- I go to clubs (Bridge hears and turns slightly while changingCD's)
Michael- WORD! Like where you be going
Mr. Bridge- (cutting the convo, as he walks over slapping Michael on the back of his neck) MICHAEL, clean up those wires and tape
Michael- (running back, head twisted) Yo I'll talk to you tomorrow IIGHT!
Nelson- yea, alright

Teacher confronts him

Mr. Bridge- you have quite a rep
Nelson-Rep?
Mr. Bridge- kids in my homeroom talk about your steps
Nelson- its only cause I go out, I'm really not all they make me out to be
Mr. Bridge- with all the heckles you get (glancing at Abdul) I'd say its quite an accomplishment
Nelson- thanks I guess, but my favorite thing is to act, tho'I know this show is jus'dance
Mr. Bridge- well your part is pure movement, I already worked the acting for the lefties, (obvious thinking) talkies will still have to move some point in another and I need a second choreographer slash tutor if you will, to pull the load till February (staring) can you assist
Nelson- sure I'll help, if you need me

They both see several of the preppy kids, including Danielle, who are mostly going to act in the show, dancing badly on stage

Mr. Bridge- (sarcastically) you know patience is a virtue (getting up) I hope you got time (leaves to get kids off top)

Nelson- yea, I got time! (One of the girls fall off) hopefully enough

Dannielle jumps down to help Farooz onto her feet

Farooz- Danny you saw that! I almost killed myself
Dannielle- (laughing) looks like we're going to need some help (she glares at Nelson walking out)

Camera focuses on Danielle's eyes and goes into her pupil, for when she blinks the scene shifts into grey skies, angling down towards two tiny figures amongst an urban park through leafless trees, to basketball court on Clinton DeWitt.

Cristian is dribbling ball with Seph to one of the courts

Alec is already there sitting beneath a hoop

Seph- What time you get here
Alec- nine
Seph- nine that's early, your voodoo mom rooster wake you up
Cris- (cuts between) may I finish my joke soul brothers
Alec- Yes I get up that early and no you may not...
Cris- (cuts in again) Well there were two WOPS walking into Tompkin square park with a ball and one of the Day-go's spots a chinese guy under the hoop, he calls out to him "Hey wanna shoot some CHINK! The Chinese guy picks up his shit and runs out the park. The Italian guys confused watching the guy run out, then turns and starts shooting the basketball, everytime it
 goes in it sounds like "chink, chink" Guy turns to
his buddy and say's "Fuck's his problem"
"**Seph**- that shit was mad corny

Few kids sitting on the jungle gym hop off and walk toward them. Seem to be friends from the neighborhood

Glen-What'up U,what'up Al,mutha'fuck'n COAL out hea'

110

Seph- Sup cousin, tell me bout'it, where your family
Glen- he right here

An older teen same height as Seph but with bigger arms rumbles thru, Junebug

Junebug- Seph! Ready to flush it on these fools (pointing to strangers otherside of them)
Seph- All day, like MJ two three (introduces Cristian) this my boy, WhiteChocolate
Junebug- (pound) white what? My devil from another level ! (both laugh) sup names Junebug
Cris- 'nice to meet ya
Junebug- same here (looks around) WE chink'n?
Glen- I'm chink'n, don't know'bout ch'all

The people from the otherside stop shooting and come over. Eight in all, mix of Black and Hispanic

Stranger- want play FULL court?
Cris- You got five?
Stranger-(sarcasm) yea LarryBird
Cris- my name is Cristian

Mood turns quickly from the energy strangers bring

Stranger- OK LARRY, we got five, want to run or what
Junebug- (steps infront of Cris) We only got four here
Stranger2- What you mean? They five people right there
Alec- I'll play
Glen- chill, chill (backs Al off)
Stranger2- Yo why don't you let him play, you the general manager or something?
Glen- No I ain't the manager, and you ain't funny iight
Stranger- NO he funny, he the clown get it

Stranger 2 rolls up his sleeve and shows tattoo of clown face on forearm

~Tension

Cris- (Breaks the tension) OK, OK, OK, (sarcasm) hahaha, your ball or ours
Stranger 2- OH LarryBird's talk'n again, something about balls (pause) SACKS-ZUH

At the point of Stranger 2's repeat insult on Cris, another teen can be seen making his way to the court

Richie Conelly the tallest of the group runs over with helmut from football field, he's known as a triple threat athelete in the neighborhood, playing three different sports and able to signature with both hands

Richie- (Brand new) Yo Junie, need a fifth?
Stranger- *JUNIE* tha's what they call you round'hea!
Junebug- Don't worry bout' what they call me, jus worry' bout gett'n yo ass BROKEN IN TOES-TITO (Glen cracks up)
Stranger- I don't think you want to make it like that papi
Junebug- yea, papi wanna make it like that, BIG DADDY wanna' make it like that all day (blank stare) Get your five on (turns to Rich) Richie you 'N?
Richie- sure

Suddenly there's an audience, a mix of children, parents and other young teens that live around the way, waiting for the game to begin, as Cristian's uncle a detective walks over pulling him aside and whispers to him

Cris's Uncle- Nephew you know these guys is dealers
Cris- can I still play
Cris's Uncle- maybe, hold on champ
Cristian's uncle goes over to one of the dealers. He doesn't come back for a while

Seph- Cee, what your ol'man and them say'n
Cris- don't know
Glen- I don't like that kid (staring at Stranger2)

Cristian's uncle returns and brings him to the side

Seph waits a moment then see's Cristian walk back to the huddle as the dealers come over to talk to his uncle again

Cris- he says they sell
Seph- Base?
Glen- softiest, pussiest, crack dilla's I eva'seen
Seph-Shhh, he's coming back
Cris's Uncle- Nephew, you always had good skill, although I haven't seen you chink's in a while, would you say you've gotten better
Cris-Why?
Cris's Uncle- They claim they want to play for the court
Junebug- For the court!?
Glen- you mean if we win they can't sell here no more
Cris's Uncle- Yeah, but if you's lose, you can't beat up the fiends no'more, they say it scares them from coming back to buy thier product.
Richie- You kidd'n right (stunned)
Seph- if we stop fuck'n up them zombie's (pulls up his hoodie) it gonna be demon night out hea'
Cris's Uncle- look at all's these kids (they stare at a mix of mothers with strollers and toddlers running through jungle gym bars) some them may be related to you, some may not, but just gett'n these junkies outta'hea (look's at two junkies scratching themselves at the handball court) would that inspire you fella's enough, to pull this one out. (pause) I mean you know you can't muscle'm out, and I don't want any'a the local Kitchener's gett'n tossed in the birdcage for tweek'n on any'a these scumbags
Junebug- my cousin got stabbed by crackhead'year ago for five dolla's, now he gotta live with a glass eye. Damn right I wanna get them Base'Heads outta'hea

JuneBug and the rest seem inspired

Seph- I'll help
Glen- let me D that Jiggaboo right there (points at stranger 2)
Cris- (Hollers at dealers) WHAT YOU'S WAIT'N FOR? YA
CHINK'N OR WHAT! (nods at uncle) see you after the game
Cris'sUncle- give'm hell

Everything goes slow motion for the first sequence.

During this effect a player yells out "Shoot for
rock". A ball is seen thrown to Glen, which he shoots
from the foul line, missing.

Game begins

Instantly dealers let it be known that there will be no
nickel-dime fouls called.
Seph takes a blow right to the jaw from an elbow, clearing out a
rebound from a missed shot

Seph- Oh that's how you wanna play (evil smile) ok, we can
play like that

Seph goes up to block a shot on the other end
ramming into a dealer coming down

Stranger- YO! What the fuck! (calling for stoppage) HOLD UP!
Stop ball, stop ball!
Seph- Nah! Don't stop ball, keep playing fuck that!
Stranger- Ok! We gonna play like that all the way then!
Seph-(blinders,speed talking) bla-bla-bla-bring the rock down
baby

People are now flushing the ball with authority, but most
of the dunks come by way of Rich or Junebug, while jumpshots
are keeping the drug dealers close

Glen- YO' THEY GOT THE NO LAY' UP SQUAD (screaming to his side) BEAST THESE NACHO'S, JUMP SEE-QUENCE!!

      Glen is being posted on by Stranger 2 who he has bad blood with and is fighting for position, when he blocks a hook shot into the gates

Glen- You gonna have to come stronger then that down hea POT-NUH!
Stranger2- Oh like this (gets the ball from out of bounds and beams it at Glen)
Glen - (catches it) thanks for the penny
Stranger2- (pulls out a knot) this here more then your whole family make in a year, I give you if you win, penny-shit, put money on it
Glen- (quickly) OK!
Stranger2- Hol up tho! What you gon' give me?
Glen- give you my left nutt bitch!
Stranger2- okay, (flashes a hand razor) DEAL
Junebug- Hey homie, you mind gett'n that out my cousins face
Stranger2- (putting away razor) we made a bet, jus want to know what I'm gett'n if I win
Glen- you crazy nigga, I don't got crack money, fuck you think I'm SLANG'N!
Stranger2- then give me your kicks
Glen-WHAT!
Stranger2-KICKS, sneakers
Glen- man you crazy
Stranger2- am I now (serious) if you win I give you this (shows knot) if I win you walk home clubfoot
Glen- (silent atmosphere) FINE, jus have my grip when we done
Seph- finished wit your soap opera?
Stranger2- (grin) yea (hawks Glen) yeah
Seph- Lets go then, whats game?
Stranger- twelve, goin by ones, and three's is two's
Seph- coo' cool, lets go' let's go (checks ball fast) BALL IN

{Note}

1"Twelve goin by one" is basically any shot that goes through the hoop is one point, except a three pointer, any shot beyond the three point line is two points.

2"Setting Picks" in the game of basketball refers to a man who stands in a spot where you are running blindly and waits for you to run into him. Because most players are so focused on their assigned man, they are unaware of the human obstacle waiting for impact. While the one setting the "PICK" is braced for contact, the one running, hits a human wall. *Other notable words for "Pick" are "Block" and "Screen"

3"Isolation" The full court game of Basketball consists of ten players in total, five on one side and five on the other. "Isolating" someone basically means there is a mis-match in one of the five positions. Most of the time the mis-match is height, a person who is taller then the other can easily get high percentage shots (easy points) over someone shorter. So the team gets the taller guy the ball and moves away from him, thus creating "Isolation"

A series of dirty plays begin to unravel from dealer's squad. A mix and mash of trips, elbows, low bridges, and dirty blocks frustrate the youngsters as they plummet to a score of nine to five

Cris- (screaming at Seph after he's picked off, and his man shoots but narrowly misses) YOU GOTTA CALL THOSE OUT MATE!
Seph- How when I can't even see that shit coming, and that SCREEN is illegal, he movin
Cris- I don't care, jus gimme a warning !
Seph-WARNING!

Junebug- (see's the game slipping away) time out' timeout!! hold ball! (huddles the group up) look these nigga's ain't shit, they jus sneaky, no jump'n ass muthafucka's (looks at Richie) Rich if we ISOLATE you on that sickly thing (camera zooms to tall but chicken boned male) think you could put that dude on smash?

Richie- oh I'm glad you finally noticed (sarcasm)

Junebug-huh?

Richie- Come on man, I been call'n for that like all day, you tell'n me you fella's jus noticed?

Glen- my bad yo, I know I been hog'n it

Junebug- only MJ get away wit one for twentyfive, down hea, we gotta share cousin

Glen- iight (gives a pound to Rich)

Junebug- Yo rich I'm gonna give (forgetting) yo what's your name again?

Cris- Cristian (smirk)

Junebug- rich I'm a' let Cris feed you the middle, think you could go to work

Richie- pal that's what I been askin'for, ISO'ISO and lets CIRCLE JERK these "NIGGERS" the fuck outta hea! (pause) no offense ←

Junebug, Seph, and Glen- NONE TAKEN

The game now takes a frantic pace, as the youngsters match dirty play with pure youthful ferocity

And it shows

One jumper lands out of Glens hands which brings the score to six, nine (6-9) after which he is eyed by his cousin, acknowledging the plan they just laid

Glen- I'll pass it, I'll pass it!

117

Flashes of a young Kevin Mchale is seen through Richie's slick   post up fakes and jukes, turning into score after score of come back vengeance

Richie- (getting his man in the air with a head fake then a drop step to the left, he racks up again) FUCK OFF ME CRIZ'NAK!

The score is quickly tied at ten

Stranger- (gasping for air) TIME OUT!

Dealer's call out

Junebug- what ya'll wait'n for?
Stranger- (hand on knee) for my man
Junebug- what?!
Stranger- (raises up) MY ACE

Coming in from out of bounds clearly the tallest of both sides a young Black male walks toward the crew and replaces Caesar, (stranger one). They call him Tyson

Tyson- (speaking to the dealer that was abused *MEANING SCORED A LOT OVER* in the post by Rich) who's that white boy there?
Stranger 4- I don't know papi (gasping) I can't make play wit'heem
Tyson- shut' fuck up

Tyson pushes him aside and gets into position

Tyson- let me get middle
Stranger 4- we no play jong-cheer (JONG* what he's trying to say is ZONE as in "we no play zone here")
Tyson-we are now (pulls him left) you get that flank and guard it with your life

Stranger 4- where chew' go

Tyson- I got this middle, anything get past you, I'm send'n it to the river (stares at Rich)

Richie once again gets the ball in the post, this time realizing a seismic difference, he tries for an up an under and almost gets blocked, he grabs the rebound and tries to back his man down.

Stranger 4- Trap, Double! (running over to help)
Tyson- No DOUBLE! I got THIS!

Rich rams into the chest of his opponent, creating a little daylight, then goes up for a shot

It's punched

The ball lands near midcourt, where a cherrypicker awaits going in for the easy bucket

SWISH nothing but net

> ~Dealers
> Point
> Match

Glen-FUCK!

Right after the inbounds, an unwise baseball pass by glen is picked off

Junebug- WHAT THE...? GLEN!!!

Stranger 2 picks up the ball and waits for Tyson running down, trailing is Richie

Seph- (screaming to Cris) GRAB THAT NIGGA, FOUL HIM!

     Cris reaches for stranger 2's arm but to no avail the pass is lobbed and Tyson is already at lift off, Richie jumps too but is lost in Tyson's shadow

    Tyson- (Flushing right on Richie's head) learn to use the N word properly (walking away) BREAD CRUMB ←(P.117)

    Dealers run onto the field, jump for joy, as Glen takes off his shoe tossing it in the Hudson

Glen- (staring at the dealer) Go fish Faggot
Stranger2-(evil grin) we already did

    Cris's uncle walks toward them but Cris turns away and walks the opposite direction.

    Wickedly slow, an eerie feeling fades the scene

    DrugPushers...TRIUMPHANT

    Camera follows Cristians' back as he leaves the grounds, while crowds of children run past him. One of the toddlers has on a red and burgundy jacket, which is zoomed in on, blanking out all view. Thee view then returns to a cup of black coffee, where cream is swirling into a transforming light brown. The stirring is done by a girl standing next to her friend amongst a backdrop of teens. It's Farooz and Danielle in a bagel shop with other students from Oxford, S.P. eating and being loud.

    Suddenly Danielle catches Nelson passing by their
    window

Farooz- (running out to Nelson, no coat in Winter) Hey SUSHI
boy!

Nelson- YES

Farooz- my friend wants to talk to you (guides eyeball to glass where Danielle's sitting) interested?

Nelson- bring'er out (glancing over)

Farooz- No come inside, can't you see its, UM FREEZING

Nelson- I know it's UM FREEZING, but I rather stay UM OUT (Nelson glimpses the preppy kids in the store, clearly it's not his crowd)

Farooz- (sticking her head in the store) Danny! He's being DIFFICULT

Danielle- (laughing, runs out) Excuse me aren't you supposed to help us lefties learn the moves

Nelson- Ok, what the hell are we talking about?

Danielle- I need help with some of the steps we learned yesterday, can you help me

Nelson- Yea, when we go to rehearsal

Danielle- and if I don't get it at rehearsal (cute attitude)

Nelson- (hypnotized, off subject) did I see you before?

Danielle-at the auditorium

Nelson- I mean before that?

Danielle takes a while to answer

Danielle- Are you late sometimes

Nelson- Alot, why

Danielle-(beat) nothing

Another long silence, and the staring into one another becomes powerful

Farooz- (breaking the tension, windshield wiping Danielle's eyes) Hel – Lo – Oh, Danny, earth to Danny, come in!

Out of left field, Nelson stomps right over to Danielle forcefully

Nelson- Gimme your number

Danielle- uh, Farooz, (uneasy) pen

Farooz- (shocked) WHAT?

121

Danielle- (eyes wide) A PEN, you know, that thing you write stuff with
Farooz- ha (beat) ha (handing her a red bic)

Nelson sticks out his left palm

Danielle- You want me to write on your hand?
Nelson- don't worry I'll make sure all the homeboys get a good look before I wash it
Danielle- (long silence, Farooz is also stunned) what?
Nelson-(cracking up) just fuck'n wit'cha
Farooz- WHAT!?
Nelson- nothing, just give it to me already before you call the five'O on me
Danielle- five oh?
Nelson- (giggling) your phone number Danielle, unless I scared you out of it
Danielle- no, not at all (tagging on hand) jus didn't understand what the hell you were talking about
Farooz- (smug, crossing arms) yeah, me neither
Nelson- look we have to work on our communication (eye to eye gesture with Danielle)
Farooz- (looking up) oh brother
Danielle- Communication, good
Nelson- (walking away) good

_Scene fades

@ }—'--,----------------   8

THE SUNKIST STAR

Int- Seph and Cristian in a diner talking about the game, when
Nelson enters

Cris- I tried to tell you to forfeit the game when that man jumped in
Seph- How you forfeit a game yo? We had nigga's come in and out
when we play all the time
Cris- Not when there's money involved
Seph- money what? (being passed a milkshake by waiter)
Cris- A bet smart guy, a bet

Nelson comes in from the snow and flops down carelessly

Seph- Damn nigga take off yo shit!
Nelson-(taking jacket off) TOUCH-EEE!
Seph- Don't you see the silk tops I got on bitch (wiping off "RunDMC"
tee shirt)
Nelson- alright'alright, sheesh
Seph-WATCH YOUR STEP OK
Nelson- its jus threads, Cris fucks wrong wit'your GIRL'here
(glances at Seph)
Cris- we lost a game at Clinton Park yesterday
Nelson- is that all
Cris- more then that partner (Nelson reaches over to take a sip of
Seph's milkshake) fuckin zombie kings made a deal wit us if they
win, they get to keep the park filled with CRIZ'NAX

Nelson- So? (vanilla mustache) just terrorize them fiends, like we always do

Cris- that's exactly the issue my friend, the deal was to leave the fiends alone, so they could shit themselves in peace

Nelson- WHAT!

Cris- more then that, but mother's gotta see these fiends CRACK'UP with their kids running around the park

Nelson- (disgusted) how can you lose a game like that?

Seph- Man we tried! But they subbed this big gorilla nigga at the end and gangsta'd themselve's to it

Nelson- (stunned) you could sub with money on?

Seph- I guess

Cris- you can't

Nelson- what choice is there, you's have to play another one

Seph- and what...GET SHOT

Nelson- You can't SUB when you got a bet

Cris- yo look (Ana is tapping on the window with Wanda)

Nelson- fella's I gotta break

Seph- (see's his milkshake is spent) damn you fuckin gook, you downed my whole shit!

Nelson- (laughing, Ralph Cramden imitation) AHHH, SHA-DAP! (tosses a penny at Seph, which hits him on the neck)

Cris- later Nel

Nelson- lata'fellas

Nelson jumps out the diner into Ana's arms and gives her a big kiss right on the mouth, then pecks Wanda

Ana- Hey sexy

Nelson- I gotta go to rehearsal in a few, which way you's walkin

Ana- we was going to the Gap to pick up presents for Wanda aunts birthday shower, until she changed her mind and decided to go see her friend in Amsterdam

Wanda- you taking the fifty'seven Nelson

Nelson- na, I'm goin under for the'R

Ana- (turns toWanda) give me the money for the birthday shower and let me get the babycap at Gap kids, and you could go see your boyfriend

Wanda- me to see my boyfriend or for *you* (tilts her head to Nelson)

Ana- oh be quiet and go get molested already (girls laugh)

Wanda- (simmering down) Ok, but make sure it's either soft blue or lite pink, alright.

Ana- what time you think you be back

Wanda-hopefully not for a while

Ana- thought you was scared to walk through the projects

Wanda- the only thing I'm afraid of starts with a P-R-E and ends with an I-O-N

Ana- (laughter) you so nasty Wanda

Wanda- I tried being good (kisses ana goodbye) too boring

Nelson- (pecks Wanda leaving) what you guys talk'n bout?

Ana-(walking away with Nelson) two minute guys

Nelson-What?

Wanda- bye Nelson, bye Dee

Ana-bye Wanda

Nelson- Hoochie Mama talk if I ever heard one

Ana- oh like you don't like it (winking)

Ana pulls Nelson by the arm, and drags him up the block pulling out an umbrella covering both of them, as it begins to rain

Ana- so tell me how's the show coming

Nelson- (see's a girl walk by with a turquoise sweater that looks exactly like Danielle, tripping) it's all good

Ana- you ok

Nelson- (catching his bearings) I mean, we're moving way ahead of schedule

Ana- that's great! Have you guys finished the first act yet

Nelson- nah, Mr. B isn't doin it like that. He got us researching all the time periods first

Ana-time periods?

Nelson- yeah like, the Rock'n'roll era, Sixties, the Disco shit, you know, era's

Ana- that's cool, it probably gonna sell crazy tickets

Nelson- yea but, I gotta stay longer sometimes, help out the can't dance'kids'

Ana- is that why I haven't seen you lately

Nelson- (Nelson spots a young lady dressed very old for her age, walk out train station with a Menorah, he takes time before speaking again) yea I guess

Ana-(prophets gaze) Waahed'muuhes n'zuum (she leans on him and places her hand on his heart)

Nelson- huh...   ~ They kiss

Ana- I know I can't see you as much, but call me at least, don't be a shadow ok (kisses him again)

Nelson-k

Ana- bye sweet prince

Nelson- bye Ann

                                                    ~End scene

                    *   *

      Int- Mr. Bridge is on stage with kids doing scenes from the movie Grease when he notices a silhouette of a boy walk through the auditorium, running toward the stage

Mr. Bridge- NELSON, what time?

Nelson- I know, I know, I'm sorry

Mr. Bridge- DON'T BE SORRY, BE HERE, GOT IT

Nelson- got it

Mr. Bridge- Now where's the routine I told you to develop, do you have it?

Nelson- (sharply) yea, yea, I got it

Mr. Bridge- you give me work, not attitude Nelson!

Nelson- (deaf)

Mr.Bridge- GOOD

Nelson- (bites his tongue) I'll need seven girls in house left, four guys stage right, all upstage, three of the seven girls will be picked up when Michael walks downstage, beside that, the four guys with no girls will all follow Mike, but stop at centerstage when he gives them the cue

Mr. Bridge- what's the cue?

Nelson- he takes out a switchcomb and combs his hair back, then the nerd comes in, plus we're going to need two chicks on blades with trays balancing drinks

Mr.Bridge- Rollerblades Nelson? (raises his brow)

Nelson- I meant skates

Mr. Bridge- who's going to play the nerd?

Nelson- I was thinking... (indecisive)

Mr. Bridge- you can be the nerd Nelson

Nelson-what?

Mr. Bridge- you heard me (emphasizing) YOU CAN PLAY THE NERD, problem?

Nelson- but Mike's going to need a second

Mr. Bridge- what do you mean second?

Nelson- in Grease, Travolta play's second to the blonde guy

Mr. Bridge- well Mike's doing it without a second for this one, is that ok with you Michael

Mike- (seeing he better say yes) sure thing Mr.B

Mr. Bridge- (Bella and Raven walk into the auditorium late) that's good Michael, now go set up music for the first sequence

 Mike- (reluctantly) yes Mr.B

Raven and Bella are now on stage apparently late, putting on dancing shoes

Nelson- so I'm the nerd, even tho' I had to stay up all nite, getting the whole scene together

Mr. Bridge- to begin you didn't do the whole scene, you just put in the beginning, middle and end. And if I can recall, Travolta was bit taller then you

Nelson- so

Mr. Bridge- so we're trying to stay true to production here (smiles)

Nelson- but your letting Mike stay alone, that's not staying true to script

Mr. Bridge- Well, when your teacher or choreographer one day you can do as you please, but till then, just do as your told (Bella accidentally drops one of her shoes off stage near Mr. Bridge, which he not only picks up but hands back politely)

Nelson- (under his breath) all the shit I make up for this show I might as well be

Mr.Bridge- excuse me?

Nelson- nothing (takes lot of grit but doesn't complain) EVERYBODY ONSTAGE NOW! AND HERE, YOU TOO BELLA! WE'AIN'T GOT ALL DAY

Mr. Bridge- (spiteful) awfully loud in here isn't it (speaking to Michael)

Michael- (unwilling tone) yeah

Danielle looks at Nelson silently
~End Scene

Int- Kids flood out school doors as rehearsal ends, Nelson being one of the first to step out, and angrily at that

Danielle quickly goodbyes Farooz and runs up on Nelson

Danielle- Hey!

Nelson- Fuck (startles him) WHAT?

Danielle- Hey sport! (trying to brighten him) How do you keep coming up with those moves?

Nelson- jus make up stuff, I don't know, (passé) it's nothing special, anybody can do it

Danielle- If anybody can do it how come Mr. B only has one choreographer

Nelson- Michael helps him

Danielle- you know what I mean, help create the dance parts

Nelson- maybe he's a bad judge of talent, I don't know, why don't you help him I'm tired of being his whipping boy

Danielle- (grinning) He like's you

Nelson- is nerding someone up, his way of affection

Danielle- actually, I bet you'll make a great GEEK (attempt at humor)

Nelson- Yeah, I BET he'll make sure of that (slamming school door open)

Danielle- so you didn't answer my question

Nelson-what question

Danielle- you know. Why you dance so well

Nelson- Maybe I don't dance well, maybe you jus really suck

Danielle-Wow, you're a real romantic (sarcasm)

Nelson- whatever

Danielle- you know Bridge assigned you to me right

Nelson- I think not, it says Bella and Raven before it says you

Danielle- well Bella and Raven was cut from the Grease part so that warp speeds you to me (cheesy smile)

Nelson- god save us

Danielle shows him the sheet of partners he has to tutor then turns to go up seventyseventh

Danielle- (sticking her wide hips out) See you eleven tomorrow

Nelson- eleven tomorrow morning!

Danielle- yup

Nelson-but I'm goin clubbing tonight!

Danielle- (quickly speaking) well have a good time then (giggling as Nelson's bus shows up)

Nelson- (repeats) *well have a good time then* (rolls his eyeballs)

(6:45 PM)_End scene

(11:45 PM) Int~ Alec walks down toward Ana's building noticing police lights twirling red and blue on her front stoop

Paul- Damn that's fucked up
Alec- what's fucked up (jus showed on the scene)
Paul- what up Al, didn't see ya
Alec- cool'cool, what's going on?
Paul- you know that old guy that owns the Southerly health store on your boy's block
Alec- (right on cue with Chez-Co being walked out in cuffs by police) yea
Paul- Chez put a beaten on him
Alec- (suspect vibe) for real, why

Chez-Co is put in the police car and driven off followed by another. The blue and red lights die off where Nelson is walking up Ninth ave

Paul- Ellen's pregnant with his baby
Alec- shit
Paul- yea, no shit

Nelson hits the scene holding a brown paper bag covering coke bottle

Nelson- Chez found out bout' that ol' bastard fuck'n Ellen huh
Alec- (whispering) will you shut up!
Paul- What up NellyNel, and yea, how'd you know?
Nelson- (looking at Alec motioning zipper mouth) overheard ya'll walking up
Paul- damn you can hear that far
Nelson- I guess
Alec-(changing subjects quickly) WELL ANYWAY (grudge look to Nelson) is the old guy hurt?
Paul- got a broken jaw and everything (nodding) Chez's shirt was all bloodied up when I got here

Nelson- pop my sisters cherry, pop your mouth is the way it goes right

Alec- yea, you can say that again (Paul strangely looks at him) so what's going to happen to the old guy?

Paul- they're gonna DNA test him, then I guess take it from there

Alec- how sure is the DNA thing

Paul-from what I heard, like, ninety something percent

Alec- yeesh

Paul- that's exactly what he said I bet, specially when they found a tape with her name on it, who knows what the fuck he been record'n

Alec- they found a tape? (horrified)

Paul- yeah man, and the funny thing is, he don't even have any recording equipment

Alec- how you know all this (reaches for Nelson's soda and takes a sip)

Paul- my cousin's a DT in Midtown North, they're look'n for his accomplice right now

Alec- (cola shoots out Al's mouth, he hands the bottle back to Nelson and try's to look calm) really

Nelson- (looking at Al's nervous state suddenly bellows a laugh) you crazy dude

Paul- what? (surprised at Nelson's reaction)

Nelson- nothing (toning it down)

Alec- damn man, you got a funny sense of humor you know that

Nelson- you mean the kind of funnies they shoot on CANDID CAMERA

Alec- SHIT ASSHOLE! Chez-Co's sister got fucked by an old health food guy! WHAT MORE! DO YOU WANT!

Paul- (confused) uh, this is weird fella's

Luckily for Alec the member's of TNT pop out of Ana's building and switch the attention immediately before the convo gets deep.

Paul- I gotta walk my dog before he does the futon, lata fella's (he dashes up the stoop) five thousand!

Nelson is rushed by TNT

Turk- Yo, yo, yo (dragging his feet down the steps to ground level) late, later, lateness, SUP?
Nelson-my bad
Cactus- MY BAD NUTHIN, why wasn't you there at the club Brutus
Nelson- was Air Force One showed up
Turk- Shit, did they (mouth full of gold teeth) Brought the whole muthafuckin squadron (mimic's taking stripe off his shoulder) what happened?
Cactus- yeah my ASIAN, what happened?

Bobo walks out the front and yells at Nelson

Bobo- My sister says your Late! Buddy!
Nelson- tell her I'll be in minute
Bobo- okay, but you know how she get when you ain't on time chino
Nelson- you're repeating yourself
Cassius- I see you been hang'n us up for some Spanish broad
Nelson-Spanish broad?
Turk- dude, I understand you got a girl and shit (sucking his gold front) but we need you in the underground every Saturday night
Cactus- if you can't be there cuz' you too stuck on that teenage love, you got's to let a brother know
Turk- can you be there family (gold teeth larger then life) I said brother man can you be there?
Nelson- yea, I won't stand you's up again, promise

They both stare at him for a good second, before loosening up

Turk- my nigga (brushing off shoulder he took imaginary stripe off and slapping it back, making a stitch sound)
  Cactus- (pound and a hug) you better be there this time POT'NA!
  Nelson- How you's do at the Sound?
  Turk- man me answering that's, gonna make me take that stripe off again
  Timothy-we got…Bombed
  Cactus- (instantly) BOOM!

    Ana blasts through the building doors

Ana- NELSON! Didn't Bobo tell you I finished!

    Seeing they handcuffed Nelson too long, Turk and Cactus make their exits

Turk- sayonara'
Cactus- bye playboy (they both pound and fade out)
Nelson- lata… hold up! What spot Saturday?
Turk- Paladium! Ya heard!
Ana- ya'DONE! (looks that could paint a lightning cloud)
Nelson- (army salute to Turk) CRYSTAL!

    Members of TNT leave

Alec- hi ann
Ana- (she ignores Alec, and beams at Nelson) I said are you finished?
Nelson- hey girl, what's poppin
Ana- hey nothing Yoshi boy, when I make you something to eat you see me first understand
Alec- look I'm'a go ok (no one notices)

    Al turns right out view from the stoop

Ana- you called and told me your dad didn't come home last night and you were starving

Nelson-yeah…and?

Ana- so I felt for you, and made a plate

Nelson-(naïve) why?

Ana-(trying to hold back tears) I haven't seen you in so long… I jus wanted to spend some time

Nelson- don't do that (pulls out napkin from brown bag)

Ana- my Dad's been teasing me, and saying stupid stuff to my mom's all week (Nelson wiping away tears, kissing her forehead) saying I better not have kids with you cause he seen Chinese and Rican babies, and their MAD FAYO

Nelson- FAYO? What's that?

Ana-Ugly!

Nelson- (laughing) you know your dad likes to play

Ana- No, he was serious, I know he was!

Nelson- (trying to console) Look, I don't know bout me mami, but I can't think of anything coming FROM, or OUT of you that would be even close to fayo

Ana- (smiles faintly) you really mean that

Nelson- well (comic relief) except for your KA-KA

Ana- oh please, you did so well for a while too Nelson (smacking his arm)

Nelson- what! (laughing)

Ana- leave it up to you to STINK things up Yoshi!

Nelson- you don't know how much I hate that name

Ana- why cause my brother calls you that all the time

Nelson- the whole neighborhood calls me that now

Ana- I think it's cute

Nelson- yeah, well I think it's… (Nelson see's a girl in skyblue skirt walking across the street with her mother, then out of nowhere, is jerked into a crazy vision of the same child being hurried through a mob of people, wearing striped tattered clothing, with numbers stitched to their shirts AND pants, matching dirty grey caps, along a muddy cow trailed road sided by barbed fences, through a pathway leading to a blackened train pulling coal, smoked' whistling high. She never blinks, let alone lose eye contact with Nelson as she trudges through the mud, with what seems to be her family, as the train pops a banshee stop, Deathly packed)

Cab passing Ana's house, screeches to a halt at a truck rolling out

Back in the real world, two men come off their vehicles, arguing relentless in the street

Ana- Nelson! (yanked out trance)
Nelson- WHAT
Ana- are you alright
Nelson- (mute)
Ana- You went blank for a sec'
Nelson- look, gotta go
Ana- (no words to describe expression) WHAT!?
Nelson-bye

Just like that, he bolts, leaving Ana in utter confusion

_SceneFades

Int- Dannielle is home Alone, working on some kind of school work when she hears her doorbell

Danielle-Nelson! What the…(catches herself) ok danceboy, how did you find me?
Nelson-need'tah'ask'ya'sum'n
Danielle- if you want to know, I don't have any of the steps down (catches herself again) how in the world did you find me
Nelson- I'm not here to dance with you
Danielle- kay, uh, I guess I'll ask how you tracked me down later
Nelson- stalked you, can we talk (phone rings, she goes to pick up)

Dannielle can clearly be heard through the door "He grabbed you and scared my address out... no I'm alright... NO don't do THAT, I'm serious! He looks harmless, just go chew on some Godiva or something..."

She returns shortly

Danielle- You know you're lucky you're not locked up
Nelson- was that...
Danielle- Farooz, yes, and if I hadn't told her I wasn't being raped right now your tushkuh' would be in cuffs
Nelson- nothing to fear, you're too bitchy to rape
Danielle- not funny danceboy
Nelson- hate it when you call me that and I only forced her cause I had to ask you something
Danielle- Wow, FORCE an address out Roozy, show up at my house uninvited, this must be serious
Nelson- No but your'bout to be, if you don't stop playing games

They stand in the doorway for a good moment, before she opens wide

Danielle- well are we to be rumor fodder for the hallway people
Nelson- Excuse me?
Danielle- Get in dummy

Nelson steps in and realizes a clean, tidy place, dimly gold tinted, slightly old fashioned

Nelson- (looks around) I'm not use to this
Danielle- what you never been in a girls pad before
Nelson- no never (sarcasm) I been in girls houses, but... never one this crisp
Danielle- Crisp?
Nelson- jus a nice crib
Danielle- well I try (cocky) but thank you none the less
Nelson- Get the fuck outta hea!

Danielle- WHAT
Nelson- talk'n bouzhee
Danielle-bouzhee? What's that?
Nelson-rich people talk
Danielle- I'm not rich
Nelson-"WE'RE MOVIN'ON UP, TO THE EASTSIDE"
 Danielle- "TheJefferson's" whatever
Nelson- there you go again
Danielle- there's what'again
Nelson-only rich people say *whatever*
Danielle-what I can't say whatever now
Nelson-fuggedaboutit
Danielle- FUGGEDABOUDIT
Nelson- shut up (slight laugh)
Danielle- so mister street'cred, what is it that brings you to my humble abode (playfully covers her thighs, pulling down her pajama tee)

        *she makes it obvious pulling her tee down, making sure Nelson sees

Nelson- don't flatter yourself HOWLIE
Danielle- Howlie?
Nelson-whitegirl
Danielle-how rude!
Nelson- well maybe you'll think of that everytime you call me DANCEBOY
Danielle-whatever danceboy, it still doesn't answer my question
Nelson-and what's that
Danielle- well, I'm not scheduled for step tutoring today, so why are you here?

        Quietly takes her hand.

Nelson- can we sit (his energy effects her, no reason why)
Danielle- yes (she gently goes down never taking her eyes off him)

Nelson- you said you seen me before the audition, when?
Danielle- the first day I transferred to Oxford I saw you run past me as I was going to phys Ed
Nelson-I don't remember
Danielle- you was wearing a "Nippon" shirt
Nelson-(shocked) u speak Japanese
Danielle- no silly, but I do know a sun burst red and white shirt is from your country. It's the rising sun
Nelson- it is, but...
Danielle- Farooz loves Sushi and I think I been in enough of them fish bars to know a Japanese flag when I see one
Nelson-Farooz eats Sushi? Yuckmouth!
Danielle- you don't like Sushi
Nelson- It's raw fish isn't it?
Danielle- you should try it sometime, it's actually pretty good
Nelson- well maybe if I ever have the money
Danielle-it's only like twelve bucks
Nelson- can't even get that much

        A comfortable quiet sets in

Danielle- can we be serious for moment
Nelson- you're not setting me up for more, rich girl snaps
Danielle- no setup
Nelson- ok
Danielle- I don't know if you know this (pulls chain from under her tee, revealing the Star of David) but I'm of Hebrew decent

        ~Simultaneous with her veiling the star, music dives
        for melancholy strings of a violin

Nelson-that's real pretty
Danielle- papa gave it to me, said it belonged to my grandfather whom I've never met
Nelson-sorry
Danielle-are you familiar with the Holocaust?
Nelson- that's where all the Jews got killed right

Danielle- (smiles) well not all

Nelson- I mean millions'tho

Danielle-seven million, maybe more

She lights a candle

Danielle- could've been more definitely, if not for men like Schindler, other names I can't pronounce, (chuckles, then looks at Nelson) have you ever heard of man named Sugihara

Nelson- Sugi who?

Danielle- looks like someone has become totally Americanized

Nelson- thought you said no jokes?

Danielle- It's no joke, Sugihara was Japans Oscar Schindler for East Europe during World War two. Now I don't know exactly what he did at that time, but what I do know is when he left, he took thousands of us with him

Nelson-US?

Danielle- yes US, as in Hebrews

Nelson- Why would someone sided with Germans want to help you, no offense but Japan bombed Pearl Harbor

Danielle-That's exactly the point, what makes stories like Oscar Schindler and Sugihara's so extraordinary is, they show people are individuals, not mindless

Nelson- Schindler was he that German who saved all them...

Danielle- yes, and Sugihara was the Japanese, who saved thousands of Jews too, one of which was my Grandmother, for whom without my father would not have been born

Nelson- which means you don't exist

Danielle- But I do exist

Stares at Nelson, silently

Danielle- I have a picture of him

Nelson-your grandfather

Danielle- no dummy, of Sugihara. It's an old black an white but my grandmother made sure to give it to my papa before she passed away

Nelson- I'm sorry

Danielle- no worries (flips up matte) he looks like you

Nelson-(surprised) Like me?

Danielle- well you are Japanese right

Nelson- yes but not all of us look type'a'like

Danielle- (laughs) so that's not you I'm always chasing away, sneaking menus under my door, wait that's Chinese

Stares at her, silently

Danielle- (grabs Nelson's hand and pulls him up, dragging him to her parents bedroom) close your eyes

Nelson- you want me to close my eyes, after you told me no jokes, and you jus re-nigged on both of'em

Danielle- oh shush'already (hands on his eyelids shuts them) now when I tell you to look, tell me what you see

Opens his palm and places a photo

Danielle-okay, open

Nelson- (looks and sees picture of an Asian man) is that him

Danielle- yup (pushes him on her bed, forcing him to sit, where she squishes right next to him)

Pause

Nelson- *he does'nt look like me* (entranced by the picture)

Pause

Danielle- on the inside, I meant (she carefully places a hand on his heart)

Nelson- he saved people (amazement)

Danielle- many people (moistens her lips)

Nelson-(quietly) true story?

Danielle- (reassuring him) true story (then looks right through him)

They kiss

Scene zooms away from the kiss, and finds its way out the room and doorway shading away slowly, fading to black   till nothing can be seen

***

@ }—‘--,-------------   9

WHO GOES THERE?

Int- Alec is cleaning his room, eating Apple slices when he finds card of lady who asked of Nelson at his play *Face turns to classic "HolyCRAP Look"

_Exeunt

Int- Alec again, this time pacing wikedly past Blimpies when he see's Seph mowing down a Club

Slams on breaks, flys in

Alec- YO!

Seph- (surprised, and choking) fuck you scream'n like I'm'cross the river for!

Alec- (gets right to it) Remember that White chick who talked to us after the play Nelson did few weeks ago?

Seph-(wiping his mouth, yellow napkins) what White chick?

Alec- Man you on crack! You know the Broadway woman (showing the card)

Seph- (squint, then wide eyed) oh no!

Alec- Exactly. Nel's gonna flip

Seph- Why didn't you give it to him

Alec- ME! You was there too nigga!

Seph- yeah, but she didn't give me the card

Alec- Yo, don't even try it, you know you was suppose to say sum'n too

Seph- whateva' man, let's just give it to him now

Alec- you heard what she said! She needed someone on the spot, right away! They prolly found a kid

Seph- yea, but we still gotta tell, plus they may not have casted that, who knows

Alec- you wanna call and see if they filled it

Seph- why?

Alec- cause if they did, Nelson doesn't have to know

Seph- (shocked) yo gimme the card (snatches it)

Alec-Chill!

Seph- what kind'a snake in the grass type'shit you talk'n. We fucked up dude, we was supposed to link that lady to HIM. You don't feel any guilt that we could've possibly fucked his chance up

Alec- I feel bad, but… (can't find words) if it's too late, its too late right

Seph slams the card on table, storming out
~ExitScene

Int- Mr. Bridge is working Nelson over again in rehearsal. Students are in Disco attire and dancing to Clyde Stubblefield's drum solo in James Brown's "Give it up, turn it loose" track

The children are not doing a good job, especially Raven and Bella

Mr. Bridge- Hold up, hold up, cut music! How many times have you rehearsed with Bella, Nelson?

Nelson- it's hard to get a hold of her

Bella- pop, pop, pop

Mr. Bridge-no excuses, how many times

Nelson- none

Mr.Bridge-how many with Raven

Raven- zilch (popping gum)

Mr. Bridge- how many times with Michael

Michael- I don't need no help wit steps!

Mr.Bridge- QUIET

Nelson- Abdul helps Michael, they live in the same building uptown

Mr. Bridge- did I ask Abdul to be a helper

Nelson- I assumed…

Mr. Bridge- don't assume Nelson, when you assume you make an ass out of yourself

Bella- Maybe if he stopped feeling up Danielle durring the weekends, us lowend chicks can get some help

Raven- we need help too *lover boy*

Mr. Bridge- is that true? You've been favoring students Nelson

Nelson- Bella and Raven can do the dances

Raven-WHAT

Nelson- they play dumb

Bella- who are you calling dumb shortee

La Tanya- I think he was talking to you BEE-OTCH

Mr. Bridge- La Tanya step outside the auditorium and wait for me

La Tanya- what I do

Mr. Bridge- don't make me ask again

La Tanya walks out auditorium, slams door

Nelson- Why am I the only tutor I can't understand

Mr. Bridge- Your job isn't to understand Nelson, this isn't a democracy

Nelson- I could use a little help

Mr. Bridge- Help? I never heard of two tutors for one student

Bella-WELL THAT WOULD BE A THREESOME

Nelson- (temper boiling) I assume if we had another tutor, he could SERVICE those SLUTS right there (stares at Bella and Raven)

Mr. Bridge- you don't use that sort of language in this school, and must I remind you again of assumptions, it's the mother of all

Nelson- mother of all what? (pause) FUCK UPS

Mr. Bridge- (standing now) Apologize to the cast Nelson and take a seat

Nelson- I feel it's you who owes me an apology

Mr. Bridge- do not disrespect me, treat yourself whatever way you choose but do not shame me or anyone else in this production

Nelson-STUPID MONKEY

Mr.Bridge-SECURITY!

Door guards Nadja and Joyce step over toward Mr. Bridge

Nadja- what seems to be the problem

Mr. Bridge- see that young man there (pointing) make sure he gets his things and is escorted out the auditorium (dark voice) indefinitely

Nelson- I HATE YOU (guards making sure to get between teacher and student while walking out) these bitches
(reffering to Bella and Raven) talking'bout my girl, while they're fingering in the girls locker! How come you never say anything when they come late, HUH?

Mr. Bridge- he is not to be let in here, understood (speaking to Joyce)

Joyce- (nodding) come on nelly, you didn't do anything really bad, YET (opening the door for him) lets be smart and keep it that way

Nelson- This show sucks anyway! IT SUCKS MAN!

La Tanya watches Nelson storm out

LaTanya- what happened?

Ignores her and bangs the door open to the street

Ana runs out pizza'shack hole in the wall, unaware of what just happened. Nelson does not care. She walks over hands full of a meal

Ana- Hey chinito'calindo! (holding slice with mushroom and peppers one hand, Coke-Cola sparkling in other)

Nelson-(menacingly) what

Ana- it's your (starting to see his mood) *favorite*

Nelson- so

Ana- what'sup?

Nelson- (looking down sitting on fire hydrant in front of the school) nothing...why you here?

Ana- what you mean why I'm here?

Nelson- you never came to my rehearsals before

147

Ana- I wanted to surprise you wit some goodies, you know you don't eat right so I thought you might be hungry

Nelson- well I don't feel like eating right now (looking down the block)

Ana- you ok?

Nelson- (totally off the subject) how long you been here?

Ana- like, ten, fifteen minutes...why

Nelson- have you seen... (pause) forget it

Ana- seen who?

Suddenly Nelson spots a girl with a red Oxford shirt on, and Farooz stand up from the pizza store Ana just came out of, leaving abruptly. The one in the Oxford gym tee gives a quick glance at Nelson before speeding away

It's Danielle

Nelson- SHIT, why didn't I see them!

Ana-seen who

Nelson- They prolly heard everything we said

Ana- (Instantly turns across the street and looks around frantically but Farooz and Danielle have already turned the corner) HEARD EVERYTHING, who are you talking about?

Nelson-WHY DID YOU COME HERE

Ana- (starting to cry)

Nelson- Oh not this again

Ana- I try so hard for you and you treat me like shit!

Nelson- Get the fuck outta hea' you're fucking things up for me

She slams pizza flat on floor, cheese side down and throws cup of soda at Nelson. He moves his face but stomach and lower pants is splashed

Nelson. Wet. With soda pants and shirt

Ana- I'm sorry I didn't mean to...

He turns and walks

Ana- (running beside him) I'm sorry, I'll wash it out (fervent, she grabs his arm) NELSON PLEASE!

Ana is frozen when she sees the look on Nelson's face, almost murderous

He continues to walk slowly down the block, leaving Ana stuck to the very pavement of which she stands

Scene fades like a turned page~

Int- Alec, Seph, and Cristian are all sitting in Blimpies sharing a large double B

Seph- I don't give a fuck what you say, we're not playing wit the Ouija in my house
Alec- why do we always gotta play that spooky shit in my crib
Cris- cause you're the only one with a moms that spooks the ghosts
Alec- (sarcasm) very funny
Cris- thank you'thank you, I'm here all week
Seph-how'bout the laundry room in my building
Alec- nah, too dirty, plus its Africa hot down there
Cris- you guys could come to my house this weekend, my mother's going to UK for few days
Seph- word
Cris- no problem (leans over to grab Seph's sandwich) you gonna finish that
Seph- take it, take it (hands the unfinished portion to Cris) want me to bring a bottle of wine
Alec- cool by me playa
Seph- I'm asking C, it's his house, brother
Alec- I know, bra-tha
Cris- bring it, I'll bust out the crystal
Alec- crystal?
Cris- (tongue in cheek) fancy glasses
Alec- cool

~Scene flashes forward to Friday night

        Int- (Cristian's apartment) *Apartment walls is covered inch by inch with mirrors. Seph and Cristian are standing on the balcony showered by city lights, and surrounded by green bottles

  Cris- Seph, you ever get that feeling that no matter how much you try to fit in, you'll always be alone
  Seph- what you mean

       A cool breeze comes and they both silence for a moment

  Cris- you know where I go to school right
  Seph- Currys, private school

Alec opens the balcony door slightly and peaks his head in, interrupting convo

  Alec- Nel said he can't make it
  Seph- what? This the second week he not wit us
  Alec- say's he has to dance at the Sound, back up Cas and his boys
  Cris-TNT?
  Alec- yea
  Cris-He can't call knee'body?
  Seph-(agreeing) right!
  Alec- well, whatever, I gotta take a shit, which bathrooms the one I can't use
  Cris- don't use the one in the bedroom, it don't flush good
  Alec- cool (he slams the fragile door)

  Cristian and Seph stare at each other as to say "Hey dude... glass breaks"

Cris- well anyway, back to what I was getting at before we were put on blast (speaking of Alec) the kids at Curry's don't take to me well, catch my drift
Seph- what, you think they should or something
Cris- it's not that, it's just, you think because I'm white and they're

white, we'll be kick'n it in the shade twenty four seven, but it's not like that'all

Seph- well, most kids in my homeroom are black or hispanic, and I think they all pussies and better keep they mouth shut

Cris- you mean slap the taste out their mouth

Seph- that too

Cris- I have absolutely no friends where I'm supposed to be like Mr. Normal, but have company in my home where I'm the odd man out, does that make any sense to you. I mean you're probably famous at your school, just cause you're Black and play football

Seph- I don't have friends in one-O-four, I hate all those faggots, SHIT I'm closer to you and Nelson then most people in my family, let alone my color

CRIS- you don't think that's strange?

Seph- look, when you die, you dyin alone, ain't no one coming with you, whether they look like you or not, you come in alone and you go out dolo, so, I think life in terms of everything BUT looks, cause even if somebody looks like you, doesn't mean they give a fuck, and that's real human nature for yo'ass

Cris- I guess we're all we got

Seph-(emphasizing Cris's words) WE ALL WE GOT, THAT'S FOR DAMN SURE

Alec- (barges in) oh man, was that a BIG'DONG I took

Seph- do you have to advertise it nigga

Cris- you guys want to head in and open up the Ouija (pushing Alec aside to step in)

Alec-can't say excuse me Ma'Sah

Seph-Come on Kutaa-Kentay

Cris-(playful English accent) I'm get out mums'Egyptian crystal, for the ghost hunt

   Mirrors of the apartment make muiltiples of everyone stepping into the room, after which a blank painting on the wall falls but none hear it

Few moments later the boys enter again. All three are sitting around table, Ouija centered, with their index fingers upon the oracle. There's also deck of playing cards edging the board

151

Full bottle of wine sits empty

Seph- Okay next time you push this thing Cris, I'm throw'n your cat out the window, deal
Cris- first off it's A-hole
Alec- Am not!
Cris- second, throw Shadow out the window (Cristian picks up his cat) you're next to follow

Seph- okay now you gett'n a little too bold
Alec-(see's something) yo
Seph- this ain't a movie dog, nigga's don't let Gap kids toss them twentyfour stories through a window
Alec- yo
Cris- just don't touch my cat, savvy?
Seph- fuck is a savvy?
Alec-YO!
Seph-(turns hard) What!

Ouija board has many symbols, one being pair of Moon and Sun

Alec- I swear that oracle was on the moon last time we got off
Seph- so
Alec-look now

Oracle sitting on top playing cards

Seph- you put that there
Alec- no one touched it, serious
Seph-serious lying
Cris- no, he's not
Seph- Cris, you put it there
Cris- (flips bird) my hand was on it the whole time
Seph-the oracle
Cris- no deck of cards, till just few seconds ago
Seph- ridiculous man

Suddenly the VCR in Cris's room turns on and starts
to play old black and white cartoons of crows

152

Cris- (tense) oh… kay (cautious touch) I think we had enough Ouija for one night, what you think

Alec- (staring at Cristian's cat which is glued on the ceiling with its fierce yellow eyes) dude your feline's trippin

Seph- let's ask more questions

Alec- I don't know (nervous)

Seph- Stop bee'n a pussy and get on it

Alec- my moms was tell'n me something bout… (cut off)

Cris- I thought ya'moms was the voodoo queen who invented this

Seph-(laughing) she probably   in there right now, (mimicking spookyJamaican accent) AL'X'MON, COME GET THE JERK OUT ME ASS, DEAD DREAD

Alec- fuck off!

Seph- come on man I'm jus joking

Alec- I'm serious dude, I don't want to mess wit this

Cris- Al will you get your fingers over! It ain't no fun wit two people (trying to be nice) pretty please, if that'll help ya fuck'n face

Alec- iight, but if something bad happens don't say shit

Seph- just get on

They all place two fingers on oracle and warm up by rotating it around the board

Cris-Weeeeeee!

Seph- feels like we're rub'n a CLIT

Alec- I don't know dude (still nervous)

Cris- what, your mom's gonna CUM squirt on us

Seph-(laughing) Cris, that's cold

Alec- (concentrated anger, and it shows) its ok, cause we all know Cris's mom is an White Euro TRASH

Which make Cristian and Seph crack up even louder, knowing that he's really jarred

Seph- ok'ok, no more talk bout nigga's moms, iight (looks at Cristian almost comical)

Cris- but it so fun!

Alec out pure stress asks direct question to the table

Alec-WHO'S GOING TO DIE FIRST

Cristian and Seph are startled

Seph- relax
Alec- I SAID WHO'S GOING TO DIE

Suddenly the oracle forcefully pulls hands to the yes
sign, then pulls violently to the letter N

It takes a noticeable deal of effort to release their indexes,
but all pull off eventually in union, rubbing thier fingers brashly,
which smell strangely of smoke'd copper. When they look back at
the Board, they see the oracle somewhere other then when they last
saw it. It is now on the number 4, and whats even more odd, is the
fact that the crystal in the center has cracked and three jagged
lines can be seen etched, rooting from each fingerprint

Dead silence

Cris-FUCKS YOUR PROBLEM
Alec- I thought you wanted to hunt for ghosts
Cris- don't pull my finger IIGHT
Alec- I didn't touch your finger!
Cris- whatever dude, but grab my joints again, and see if you
don't feel the back of my hand

Seph has a puzzled look dawned on his face, as
Cris and Alec continue to argue

Seph- why did it go to N?
Cris- cause this faggot pushed it
Alec- (hears something) is that thee…
Cris- yea right

Seph- (sympathetic stare) Cris, he's not bullshitting, you know you felt it

Cris- bullshit

Seph- nobody was thinking of N, the letter N

Cris-this dumbass was (nodding toward Alec)

Seph- I know Al gets stupid sometimes but to imply Nelson's going to die first is a bit (trying to hold back) you know... evil

Cris- I don't know, talk to your boy

     Suddenly a sharp BANG, pangs cris's door

     They freeze

     Cristian bolts to the door SWINGS it open

     ~Camera shot of Cris's empty hallway, the elevator opens letting light enter the dimly lit corridor, revealing a strange shadow on the wall, then closes smoothly, taking back the light it originally gave

     Door shuts

Cris- look (low energy) I'm tired, I'm 'a call it the night fella's, you's can crash here if ya's like

Alec- who was it'

Seph- (spreading playing cards around table, pulling a Jokers'Tally'Ho) SOMEBODY KNOCK?

     Goes to room then turns

Cris- nobody (closes door)

End
Scene

@ }—'--,--------------   10

RAINSONG

{Note}

Within this book from time to time the reader will encounter references to the drug known as "Crack Cocaine". The reason I have written about this narcotic and time when it was distributed, is because of the way it changed not just my life, but the life of so many residents in the city I was born.

The neighborhoods that were low income that I got to know many of, because of my non-existant parent and friends who took me in, were so spread out geographically, that I spent many years traveling to different areas of New York from a young age. The areas I visited weren't always the prettiest but they still had a way about them, some sense of order. In example, the times where I've experienced or heard of violence directly related to me or not, were few and far between. But around the time I entered Junior High School (1988) older teens I knew in the neighborhood and even brothers of some friends were no longer alive.

Crack because of its low selling point, became a vacuum for young entrepreuners ruthless enough to bump off other "Pushers" and take their clientele. This atmosphere created one of the most violent episodes in my lifetime. I saw neighborhood after neighborhood go through transformations that I could only describe as, APOCALYPTIC. It was as if the violence of the Miami Cocaine Wars of the early 80's merged with George A. Romero's Dawn of the Dead.

The areas that were Black and Hispanic were hit hardest. Even my area which was still predominately White working class, felt the effect. But a good friend of mine (withholding name) explained to me that before "CRACK" even Uptown where he lived, families were still structured and many were graduating college and pursuing better lives. Yes there was Coke and Heroin, but those drugs were still hard to get by most financial standards and alcohol was probably the biggest addiction. But when the "five doller Crack Rock" made its home on the streets of Harlem, almost EVERY FAMILY he grew up with was affected by its nightmarish gravity.

To see girls that were Goddesses in the neighborhood, whom carried themselves with such dignity, walk the streets with defacation on their skirts, offering fellatio for six dollars or less, made him realize what this drug actually did. It was built to kill the Human Spirit. And it did just that. For lack of a better word it won, just plain conquered, it succeeded in killing physically (African American Homicide rates doubled) and maybe worse, it ate up families and souls

Int- Paul is speaking with Ana on the stoop of her building.

Paul- Sup mami, why the long face?
Ana-nothing, just stuff
Paul- well, got stuff for'ya

Paul shows Ana a graffiti mural of her name being held up by Mickey and Minnie mouse

Ana- Hey, you drew that for me
Paul- well it has your name on it doesn't it
Ana- (jumping into hug him) thank you so much (kisses his cheek)
Paul- well thought you might need a little pick me up
Ana-really?
Paul- yea, you been pretty down for a minute
Ana- boy problems
Paul- it's that CHINO again huh
Ana- he has a name you know
Paul- well you know how Jewish guys impress the Latin ladies
Ana- by speaking bad Spanish (giggles)
Paul-very funny
Ana- (still laughing) I'm surprised you got my name right
Paul- keep talk'n and watch me take back that masterpiece
Ana- no way! This'about the only sunshine I had all day
Paul- well, happy to be of service… (Paul hears loud voices and turns to see, who's arguing)

Turk and Cactus are raising hell walking toward the stoop

Cactus- YO I HOPE I DON'T SEE THAT LITTLE MUTHAFUCKA IN FEW DAYS, FEW WEEKS FOR THAT MATTER
Turk- take it easy Cas
Cactus- YOU TAKE IT EASY, I HATE THEM AIR FORCE

NIGGAS MAN! I'M TELL'N YOU IF I SEE THAT
DUDE, I'M GONNA...
Turk- what, fuck him up'he's only lil'kid
Cactus- I'll slap a little kid, I don't care

They reach the head of the stoop and walk up the
stairs, as if Paul and Ana are invisible

Turk- (pulls out a small plastic sac just big enough to hold a
quarter, which is filled with green stuff) Yo Cas (holds up
sac) I got just what you need
Cactus- Hope so, or that little Wontons gonna get his
cookie cracked
Turk- (pulling Cactus) come on nigga, stop wake'n up the
whole block, let roll this (reveals a cigar from his inner
jacket pocket and slams door shut)

Ana is mystified

Paul- your lil' man sound like he better skip town for few days
Ana- (deep thought) huh
Paul- you didn't hear just now (wide eyed) that dude looked
pissed
Ana- (muttering to herself) why wasn't he at the club tonight?
Paul-Diana...
Ana- Look (quickly) thanks for the drawing (dashes up steps to
go in) goodnight!
Paul-(stumped) nite'ma (door slams) mi

_Scene End

Int- Ms. Kietz the science teacher is not in, a substitute is
there, and Lamott, Taheem, and Craig are in the back with radio

Hermin- NellyNel! What the deal, I hear you been evicted
(lifts a flyer for the Spring performance)
Nelson- I'm better off for it too
Hermin- But you love dancing
Nelson- I love something more (takes out picture)

159

Hermin- who's that? (likes what he see's) whoa'

Nelson- yeah, the photo doesn't bring out her eyes enough, she has crazy sparkles, and left eye is silver

Hermin- silver (lights up)

Nelson- I know, I was like that too, but when I kissed her for the first time, I looked right into her and boo-yah! Sterling!

Hermin- she goes here?

Nelson- yup

Hermin- never seen her

Nelson- she in S.P. so she hangs wit the smart kids (proud of this) cool huh!

Hermin- yeah'yeah, pretty smart, can't beat that

A tune comes on the boombox from the back, Digital Underground's "Same Song" pumps from across the room

Taheem- yo, call that sucka'

Lamott- Nel smooth! Fuck ova!

Hermin lets him

The whole crew is bouncing to the bass when he gets there

Taheem hit's it off

Taheem- I came for the party, to get naughty, get my rocks on Eat popcorn, watch you move your body to the pop song that I'm singing, dinga-linging, funky beats ringing Everybody's swinging in the place _As I kick the J-A-Z-Z-Y style—R&B mixing it wit the Hip Hop swing beat— Champagne in my hand, it won't be long till I'm gone -- It's just the same' ol' song

Lamott puts on Groucho Marx glasses attached with fake mustache and nose

Lamott- It's just a freestyle, meanwhile, we keep the beat kick'n—Sweat dripp'n,girlies in the limo eatin chicken—oops don't get da'grease on your pantyhose— I love ya Rover, move ova' I gotta blow my nose— Sneezin, but still pleaz'n to all the slimmies—Pull out myJimmy, time to get busy wit'a Jenny—If it's good'n plenty don't you know— There I go, there I go, there I go—But I don't go nowhere wit'out my Jim hat— when I'm rappin, if she's clapp'n then I'm strappin cause I'm smarter than that—Then girlie maybe we can get along—Cutie after cutie it's just the same old song

They all do chorus, except Nelson who is not seen, they purposely hide him in the back, behind everybody (Taheem slides his Yankee cap off and puts it on Nelson)

Craig- MoneyB, the freaky deaky, the squeaky meaky up an down— well as a matter'a fact I'll be right back I gotta take A'leaky—So while I'm drainin entertain'n, but I got fame— And the bases I touch, too much for me to tryin to be name'n— Ay'yo, you saw me on cable and grip— I busted in and I was goin to win— Clark Gable back in Oakland it's the same old song—Sporty shorties, same freckles an hat—Drinkin the same forty

Lamott- Hypothetical,political,lyrical,miraclewhip—Just like butter, my rhymes are LEGIT—Cause I'm the Humpty, not "HumptyDumpty" but HumptyHump—Here a hump, there a hump, everywhere a humpty'hump
Taheem- Ah shut up and just listen—Not diss'n don't get me wrong— But to me its just the same old song—So just watch, cuz my name is Shock, I like to rock and you can't stop this— 2Pac go'head and rock this!
Nelson- Now I clown around when I hang around wit'the Unda-ground—Girl's use to frown, say I'm down, when I come around—Gas me and when they pass me they use to diss me— Harass me, but now they ask me if they can kiss me—Get some fame, people change, wanna liv'they life high—Same song, can't go wrong, if I play'd the nice guy

161

Lamott- Claim'n' fame must've changed now that
we became strong
Nelson- I remain stil'the same
Taheem-Why Tu?
Nelson- Cause it's the SAME SONG   **5 --**
---,-'-{@

They all do the chorus

A silhouette of a girl can be seen watching

The song ends, and the whole crew jump on him

Craig- Yo! Don't Nel look like PAC!
Lamott- I didn't know this little nigga could rap

Rakim- You nice'ya nice, but you need to give me back my
Jersey playboy
Taheem- (smiling at Rakim) nah, let'm wear that shit cousin,
jus for today (points nose at door where Danielle is standing)
Lamott- SMOOTH NEL, A PIMP MACK

They all bust out laughing as Danielle and
Nelson make their way to kiss each other

In unison

Whole Crew- OoooH SNAP!
Nelson- let me introduce you (takes her by the hand) this is Craig
and Rakim
Danielle- hi
Nelson- they cuz'n's
Craig-hello sweet thing
Nelson- Danny 'this Lamott
Danielle-hi
Lamott- (pecks her cheek) forgive me honey but I have to do this
(starts singing) "Nelson got jungle fever, he got jungle fever…"

They all laugh, including Danielle

Nelson- and last but not least, Taheem

Danielle-hi

Taheem- (gives her a hug) take care my man here (winks) he a little sensitive

Nelson- whoa, thanks... maybe

Taheem- u ain't faded (nodding) just letting her know, you the kind'all the chicks wanna marry

　　　　Danielle laughs

Nelson- ok'ok, I think we had enough pleasantries for the evening (takes her wrist) time to go

Lamott- you cutting

Danielle-he's teaching me how to be bad (winks)

They all bust out

Whole crew- OOOOOH!! GO NELSON! IT'S YA BIRTHDAY, IT'S YA 'BIRTHDAY

Right before Nelson leaves with Danielle, Taheem calls out

Taheem- Don't bend the cap!

　　　　Everyone waves them out

Danielle- nice to meet you all, bye!

　　　　Ana from the back hidden hears Lamott and Rakim playfully saying bye to Dannielle. Ana is looking fierce at the two walking with their backs turned to her, arm in arm, toward the fire exit, to cut class.

She waits a moment. Then follows

She trails them to a movie theater, where Nelson is
fumbling through his pockets

Nelson- hold on I got this, damn! Where's my money
Danielle- Here poor boy (she pulls a wallet out her purse and out comes
a twenty paying for both of them)
Nelson- sorry you have to pay my way
Danielle- PAY YOUR WAY, this ain't a charity, I'm spending for
your ASIAN TONGUE BETWEEN ME
Nelson-that's racist
Danielle- shut up! You know you want it
Nelson- yes I want it (sarcasm)
Danielle- I hope your tongues not tired
Nelson- (annoyed) whatever
Danielle- come here, you know I'm jus joking with you (pause) by the
way... can I see how BIG your FORTUNE is, when we get inside
Nelson- THAT'S IT! (Dannielle laughs while being chased)

Ana across the street. Witnessing the whole thing

*Camera close up on Ana's face breathing heavily. She
turns angrily and does not see the Mexican delivery boy on bike

Danielle runs into theatre with Nelson right behind~

Ana just misses the delivery boy, but a plate of cheesy
nachos, lands smack on her chest. When she turns to see Nelson,
he's gone, apparently into the movie with Danielle

~

E
n
d

S
c

Int- Bobo is walking toward Luigi's to get a slice when he bumps into Seph and Cristian

Cris- hey, beaner (not noticing slash on Gordos's left cheek)
Bobo- stupid whiteboy!
Seph- Looks like you been dream'n'bout Freddy again

Cris- did your gay lover treat you rough Tonto
Bobo- (throws penny at cris) no you ass, my sister is fuck'n bugging out
Seph- Sup?
Bobo- that fuck'n Yoshi's been playing her, with a white girl
Cris- (happy) WHAT, Nelson's storming the field like that (slaps Bobo on the back) your sister should be proud
Bobo- (wipes Cris's hand off) yeah, why?
Cris- cause she's dealing with a pro, that's why
Seph- get real DPS (looking at Cris) Carlos, is she really flipping out?
Bobo- does this look like she's taking it lightly (takes off shirt and shows scratch marks along his back)
Cris- (suddenly serious) she any better
Bobo- like you care
Cris- No you fuck'n idiot we was play'n OUIJA the other night and
Seph- (cuts Cris off quickly) this nigga said Ouija (laughing fake)
Bobo- Ouija, you mean like the scary board with the letters and shit?
Cris- yeah we was play'n and Al asked who was gonna… (Feels tense jerk on his collar)
Seph- GET KIDS FIRST (dragging Cris down the block)
Bobo- ANA'S PREGNANT!
Cris- that wasn't the question
Seph- (almost safely out of earshot) will you come on
Bobo- (looking confused) you guys are fucking weird
Seph- weird, I LOVE IT (just happy to split up Cristian's loose lips and Bobo's naïve ears) Love it!
Bobo- And tell Nel to give me back my knife
Cris- knife?

165

Bobo- my sister broke up wit'him at lunch today and gave him my favorite swiss knife
Cris- your sis'is crazy

Bobo flips the bird at Cris and strolls out of view

Seph- knife?
Cris- it's just a swiss army, no need to get wound up
Seph- but that is odd
Cris- it probably some senseless bullshit to get that dude thinking hours over nothing, trust me girls like to play wicked mind games
Seph- yeah! When they're like thirty, but that's pretty advanced breakup psychology for a junior high school chick
Cris- (gives seph a tittytwister) ahhhh shad up!
Seph- OW! That hurt (swings and nicks Cristian in the arm, Cris runs before seph loads up for another blow)
Cris- *break up psychology*, what kind of uppity black talk is that (Cristian ducks from a Mc Donald's cup thrown at him on the corner of 56th)
Seph- COME HERE! (starts to run after Cris, who is laughing while Seph is gaining on him)

The scene goes out while they horse around screaming in the street. Cris for some strange reason yell's "GHOSTS'OF CHRISTMAS PAST EBENEZER" at that moment the scene fades, echoeing his words

Int- Oxford Junior high
Darcy is storming out of class and into the hallway being followed by Hendrix

Darcy- don't follow me
Hendrix- come here!
Darcy- leave me alone!
Hendrix- Na'na, you say all this racist shit and now you think I'm gunna'do nutt'n
Darcy- I'll get Patrick to fuck you up
Hendrix- get that bati'bwa in my face, and I bet I whup his ass!
Darcy- you lucky I'm not coming back to this school, Black nigger

Darcy hit's the corner of the staircase entrance when Hendrix starts to bolt after her, right there Nelson comes out the doorway and grabs him

Hendrix- THAT WITCH gotta get this (put's up a fist, with four finger ring that says "Judah")
Nelson- let it go Crew (expressioning peaceful profile for persuasion) plus Five Oh' is right there on the next floor, talk'n with Evil
Hendrix- you're Lion'mon
Nelson- (put's a hand in the air) shh, listen…

Police walkie talkies tweeking and dispatch is hailing numbers and codes under the frequency, also Levi's voice can be heard echoing along the staircase

Hendrix- You know that Bitch gunna get you in some real shit one day
Nelson- I don't even talk to her no more
Hendrix- good, cuz she BLOOD CLUT (dense stare)
Nelson- I get the point (tries to smile to take the edge off) let's go friend

Hendrix is still stuck on the spot

Nelson- come on dread'lock RASTA, plus you got an education waiting for you
Hendrix-what! More white shit!
Nelson-white lies means cash money (widen's his eyes)
Hendrix- (pause then laughs) let's go budah bless (little bit warmer) and I better not see you playing tongue twister wit'that WITCH ok CHINA MON
Nelson- (raises left hand) Scouts honor
Hendrix- (laughs even louder) you know, you the first Japan I met, and you OK (put's his arm around Nelson)
Nelson-thank u

Hen's giggling can be heard down the hall, as a shade fills the floor blanking out everything in darkness, zooming in on a fire extinguisher until the fire extinguisher is blacked out with only a tiny dot left to be seen, on the word "Caution" that's written on label

_End Scene

****

@}—'--,---------------   11

2EARS1MOUTH

1 Mr. Bridge was the best teacher I had. In many ways he showed how much volume a single person can have on a kid's life, just by investing some energy and thought to his craft. A lot of weight was placed on him cause of his sexual orientaion, by students and fellow teachers, but if he was marred by any of it, certainly it never showed. A smooth operater and Wordsworth to the last... And true gentlemen

Int- Alec walks into Nelson's lobby and has a message to give to the doorman

Alec- you seen her?

Joel- you mean that fly little blanquita that just walked out with the ponytail

Alec-She came here?

Joel- Yeah, she was look'n for nelly

Alec- so I guess I don't have to give you this then (holding a letter)

Joel- if it's for Nelson give it to me, I'll give it to him when he comes in (looking at note strangely) Mr. B?

Alec- what she tell you

Joel- something'bout, tell Nel to call her when he gets in, that it was real important

Alec- then here then (passes note) hopefully you see'em

Joel- don't worry my shift ends in an hour, but I'll pass it to NightHawk

Alec- girl got AZZ

Joel- Yeah, and those hips look like chuleta's already, that chino got Ana and a white big booty girl check'n up on him (polishing knuckles) I taught him well

Alec- fuck outta hea, it was my playa tutor'n that got him ON IT

Joel- With jeans that say "FreshlySqueezed" I doubt it

Alec- for your information I bought these for Julie...

169

Frank the superintendent walks in with Daily news in hand, as Joe pretends to do his job

Joel- OK, MAKE SURE HE GETS IT (flags letter boldly) thank you sir, let me get this door
Alec-(walks out) thanks
Frank- (opens up Newspaper he walked in with) You see this shit (showing front page) Little girl California walk into school and shoot two people right here (bangs his chest) shoot teacher first (gesture) she die right there, other person she shoot (shows picture on desk) only fourteen old, hospital now, don't know if she make it (shakes head) oh my god
Joel- it's not like when we were growing up Frank
Frank- you can say'a that again
Joel- back then if you had problems, you would shoot a fair one. Now their jus'shoot'n
Frank- Yeah and they replace hand for Boo-lets
Joel- getting younger all the time too

~Scene end

Int- Bridges classroom, the class is dark, shades are full down and a shot of the globe is closed up on

Nelson- Why am I here?
Mr. Bridge- the question isn't why you are here (pause) the question is why you are not in my show
Nelson- you fired me remember
Mr. Bridge- you fired yourself
Nelson- Look how you treated me!
Mr. Bridge- do you feel you were treated unfairly (smiling)
Nelson- ABSOULUTELY
Mr.Bridge- describe absolutely
Nelson- Raven comes late all the time and you never say anything bout'it
Mr.Bridge- And?

170

Nelson- AND… it's not the same for me

Mr. Bridge- is that all that's not fair
Nelson- Bella comes in late more then Raven, and on top of that she doesn't do shit for the show
Mr. Bridge- watch your language young one (no humor)
Nelson- she doesn't do anything right, EVER
Mr. Bridge- and you're wondering… (examining his nails, nose up)
Nelson- why you never say anything to them, but when I come in just two or three minutes over, you go off on me like knives is cumm'n'out'ya'eyeballs

Mr. Bridge opens his desk and brings forth what seems to be 4 thin pieces of wood shaped like a man. He then puts the 4 thin pieces together and it takes the shape of an Oscar, like that of thee Academy Awards

Mr. Bridge- My husband is from a very cold place
Nelson- the ghettos rough
Mr. Bridge- (left eyebrow raised) Northern Europe Nelson, I know I'm black but not all of us live in Hogan's Ally
Nelson- I thought gays can't get married
Mr. Bridge- we were married in Denmark
Nelson- so you have a husband… Who's the wife?
Mr. Bridge- (Ignores this) My husbands Pagan
Nelson- like a devil worshipper?
Mr. Bridge- No, like a Pagan. (pause) Anyhow his family roots are from an old line of Viking blood, so naturally he tells me bedtime stories… most of them are rather gruesome I admit, but one must say they were... (suddenly quiet then) SKIOBLAONIR!
Nelson-(spooks Nelson) Skee'oh what?
Mr. Bridge- It's a boat in Norse Myth that cannot sink and sails always to its destination
Nelson- so you called me here to speak of boats (the teacher ignores this)

Mr. Bridge- now the boat was not created by hands of men but by the hand of FREYR, Norse God of Manly Pleasures

171

Nelson-Manly pleasures?

Mr. Bridge- but he was also God of harvest, meaning food from the earth, trees. (pause) Now legend says that he can touch a tree and tell if the wood within can make for a good boat. Can you touch a piece of wood and tell if it's quality?

Nelson- guess not, but why would I need to, I've never made a boat, and probably never be sailing anywhere

Mr. Bridge- (grins) you're sailing right now Nelson (pause) but the ocean you're travelling is life, Ocean of Life, get it. Now I'm not a GOD but I know a good piece of wood (touches Nelson) when I feel one

Nelson- why do you always get on me in rehearsal, like why can't you give it a rest, like why…

Mr. Bridge- Freyr also says a man should never ask WHY (Nelson is silent at this because he just said why repeatedly) I mean after all, Freyr is a Big DICK Phallic God so I would say if he says "WHY" is a nagging, weak punk'ass word I would listen, YES Nelson?

Nelson- uh yea

Mr. Bridge- and I heard from some of the girls (Darcy) that have detention with me that you're not bad in the SIZE department, so you should think of being what you're supposed to be and leave the word "WHY" for thee'ungifted

Nelson- not bad for Chink

Mr. Bridge- oh please, there's plenty of STRAPPING Asian men, I bet that stereotype was made by a guy with a flea cock. But getting back to the BIG picture (Bridge takes apart the wooden Oscar to it's original 4 thin pieces) the mighty boat that FREYR made unsinkable is not made from the Hardest Oak or a tall tree, but from thin weak pieces of wood, layered on top of one another (puts wooden Oscar back together) do you know why he did this?

Nelson-no clue

Suddenly Mr. Bridge yells

Mr. Bridge- SKIOBLAONIR! (Nelson looks lost) come on say it

Nelson-what?

Mr.Bridge-SKIOBLAONIR!

Nelson- SKIO-BLAONIR!

Mr. Bridge- good (gives Nelson the Oscar) now you know when I get on you it's just chopping you down, but like Freyr I only chop you down to raise you up (winks)
Nelson- good wood
Mr. Bridge-(pats Nelson's head) not bad

Mr. Bridge turns his face to the windows and speaks without looking

Mr. Bridge- you know the Vikings were sea faring people and had to find new lands to survive, it was not a choice. As is for you, the destination is not going to come as you please, BUT... if you can bring it all together, like four seasons in a year (taps Oscar in his hands) you will be MAN my SON
Nelson- my ship, is it unsinkable
Mr. Bridge- only time will tell... now go

Nelson leaves the room hearing an invitation

Mr. Bridge- rehearsals don't start at four anymore, they start half hour earlier
Nelson-three thirty?
Mr. Bridge- YES (cracks faintest of smiles, but it's enough to let him know he's back in)
Nelson- Yes (uncomfortably) yes sir that is
Mr. Bridge- Make sure the guards see that when you come thru (points at wooden Oscar in his hands)
Nelson- ok (leaves)
Mr. Bridge- One more thing Mr. Obikane
Nelson-(sticks his head back) what's that Mr. B, I mean Bridge
Mr. Bridge-DON'T BE LATE
Nelson- never again sir
Mr. Bridge- Cheerio (snaps head down to paper he's grading)

Nelson leaves echoing a large whistle through the hallway, which can be heard in Mr. Bridge's room, where he's smiling unusually broad for grading papers

_SceneEnd

Int- Danielle is sitting at Shandon Star, a pub which is older then her grandparents, which specializes in brisket beef sandwiches

Danielle-You're back!
Nelson- that's right! (taking a sloppy bite, of his gravy drenched sandwich)
Danielle- Boy I would kiss you right now, if you weren't mopped up in that goo

N
e
l
s
o
n
-
how
did
you
kno
Al
was
my
friend
when
you
gave
him
the
letter

Danielle- I didn't, I was walking to your building when, this tall kid just ran up on me (remembering main detail) OH I was wearing the Oxford Gym shirt, and said "HEY YOU KNOW A KID NAMED NELSON, CHINESE
Nelson-(laughing) What!

Danielle- and I was like, (snooty tone) he's Japanese by the way

Nelson-(beyond laughter) YOU DID NOT!

Danielle- (not seeing why this is funny) yes I did, and he apologized and I gave him the letter to give you

Nelson- Girl you are CRAZY (trying to gain composure) was that the first time you was down here

Danielle- down here, what do you mean down here?

Nelson-this block, you know Hell's...

Danielle- I think so, yes (staring at picture with a red bearded man pulling carriage with a mule on the reigns, titled "Drink Guiness, It Makes You Strong") that's definitely not Kosher

They stare with evil grins at each other

Nelson- (wipes off gravy filled mouth to napkin) Now feel my tongue

Danielle-(deep smile) my'pleasure

While in the midst of beautiful moment Seph and Cristian barge in, sweat drenched, Seph tossing football in hand

Nelson- Hey fella's

Cris- well,well,well, speak'of the Devil! (Grinning)

Nelson- Come here if you want to find out, you cheesyMick

Cris- Dutch by the way (pulls up seat then goes to the bar) HeyPete! Toss me an iceyHiney!

A voice can be heard whistling in from the bar

Pete the bartender- you'd be lucky if trew'you's a doctor pepper, yuh'little prick'you!

Camera pans back to Nelson and Danielle

Nelson- and this my brother

Seph- surely, you can tell (joke)

Danielle- I've heard lots'about you (stares at Nelson)

Seph- and I've heard alot of you (stares at Nelson)

Nelson- I'm back

Seph- back in what

Nelson- the show

Seph-in school

Nelson- yeah, and I wouldn't have been if Nerf'head wasn't around

Seph- (laughing) yeah, he tol'me

Cris- (coming back from the bar) Nelson can I have a word with you

Seph- chill out Kraut, have a seat

Cris- (wide eyed to Seph jerking his head toward front)

Seph- Nelson you're no man of fortune

Nelson-what?

Seph see's Ana and Bobo just outside glancing at the menu advertised on the window. He gets up from his chair

Seph- Cris needs you to dial some numbers for him at the phone booth

Nelson-what?

Cris- (playing along) uh, yea, I'um, broke, twisted my wrist out there (shows football)

Nelson- you looked fine coming in, you still got digits don't you (twirling his fingers)

Danielle in utter confusion

Cris- JUS WILL YOU (grabs Nelson's armpit, pulling him up) COME WITH ME

Nelson- ok, ok, easy

Danielle- I know a little first aid, I could check that wrist out if you want

Cris- (forced smile) you just sit there and enjoy the world's best brisket, Clark Kent here is goin'to help in the phone booth

Nelson is clearly irritated.
When they get to the back he's had enough

Nelson- (slaps Cris's hand off) DID YOU TURN A
SHITHEAD OR SUMTH'N, WHAT'SUP
Cris- (point's a finger in front of Nelson's nose, aiming at
the door) that's whats up

Seph is seen conversating with Ana, buying time
for Nelson's escape

Nelson-perfect
Cris-that may be an understatement
Nelson- is there a back way out
Cris- there is, but (staring at Danielle) fuck'you goin to tell   her
Nelson- (pushes Cris out the phone area) come on, I'll tell her
there's a fire or sumth'n

They do not look natural when they get back

Danielle- (concerned) is everything alright
Nelson- look we gotta go
Danelle- to the hospital, (looking at Cris) is your wrist broken
Nelson- (talking in spurts) No, there's a fire
Danielle- a fire?
Cris- yea, a fire in the basement, inside uh, the freezer
Danielle-Fire in the freezer!
Nelson-(eye's of homicide glance upon Cris)

Cris- (tries to clean it up) yea, uh, some of the pieces
of meat in there caught fire
Danielle- WHAT? How can meat inside a
FREEZER catch fire?

Seph cannot detour Ana any further. He can be
seen miming to Nelson "GET OUT"

Ana opens door finally coming in

Danielle-but I don't understand…

Cris- (resorts to force) OH ITS A FUCK'N IRISH
BARBEQUE! WHO KNOW'S IF THEY'LL
EVER GET IT RIGHT! (grab's Danielle by the
arm, kicks a couple of chairs out the way, as
Nelson holds her coat and handbag, disappearing
into the back)

Seph rushes past Ana and Bobo who's
ordering sandwiches and stares into a patch of fallen
seats and table strewn of half eaten food

SCEN E
END~

Int- Music starts "You get the best from me"
from Alicia Myers plays while next few scenes are
run thru

Bella and Raven are coming in late for
rehearsal when they spot Nelson on stage directing
steps of disco scene, nearly all the students are up.
Bella and Raven look on in disgust, as Nelson
goes over to Danielle, grabs her waist and takes
her personally through a sequence

Raven- Look at them (sucking her teeth)
Bella- hope she fall's off stage and parts with some dentures
Raven- can't believe Arsenio gave that jerk off 'another chance
Bella- (staring as Danielle gives Nelson a wink, then steps in
tight) look at her, I don't think we can call him jerkoff no more,
the way that J.A.P is working her wide ass all over his Canoli

Mr. Bridge passes behind the two

Mr. Bridge- (whispering) ladies are we dancing, or just chewing gum?
Bella-oh (startled)
Raven- we were jus observing moves from... (cut off)
Mr. Bridge- Observation is for the producer (pointing at himself) and the choreographer (waves hand toward Nelson on stage) and since neither you are either, I suggest you get to stepping
Bella- yes Mr. B
Mr. Bridge- and let's save the knitting needle conversations for the watercooler ladies
Rachel- yes Mr. B

Scene jumps to Danielle running out a Joke shop with Farooz, on rainy day

Farooz- Nelson told you to get this? (pointing at fake afro Danielle is holding)
Danielle- rightee'O
Farooz- didn't know there was a Panther party in one of the dance programs (sarcasm)
Danielle- (too happy to care) you're such a kill'JOY you know that Roozee
Farooz- (pointing at hair piece) that things ludicrous
Danielle- I know (grinning) he's going to love it

"Alicia Myers fades into "ABC" by the Jackson Five, when the sequence turns to MoTOWN.

Michael and a group of girls turn from painting a red brick wall at the back of the stage, to laugh at Chantae, Chantell, and Latanya prancing out with Beehive hair styles, then Nelson really gets them going when they see him sporting a fake Afro. They all do the dance and Abdul makes an entrance, singing little M J's part doing moves like the Jackson five. Mr. Bridge even joins in the action, as he spins and shoop's over toward Bella and Raven, giving them the cue to swing back, as Mr. Bridge slides forward, pointing to Michael who glides over and dances with Chantae, and Chantell the twin sisters. After a few more moments of Motown's finest, "ABC" is traded for "McFadden & Whithead's "Ain't no stopping us now" where all the students of the show follow Nelson up top, and on his command execute the Bus Stop. The dance is only done once, and at the snap of Nelson's Afro, everyone and everything is cut to pure silence, parylysing the auditorium. Suddenly a bold beat strikes. "Take on me" from the album "Aha" echoes loud and shots of student after student raise heads in close up view

Montague vs Capulet choreography is done in Punk rock style, with blacked out stage and lone spotlight shining down on sole dancer, taking a fraction of time during the beginning of the song. Then after each dancer has a moment of shine, the second and endpiece of the track is danced together by all students, but in an order that is broken into two groups, every now and then splicing between one another, like gangs fighting till the song's climax, with all falling on the floor united

It ends with Abdul shaking Nelson's hand centerstage, both dropping, as the curtains close between them

Mr. Bridge- (calling out from behind) I hate to say it but I think we have a hit (begins to clap alone) It is exactly six fifteen (6:15 PM) By this time next week your family, friends, and fellow student's will be shuffling in for good seats, while backstage you'll be putting on make up, and other things for your performance.
(Mr. Bridge takes a long look at the cast, then speaks out of character) They say youth is wasted on the young. And most of the time, I agree. And although its hard for you to swallow, most of you will never be filthy rich or famous (pause) But loved… *maybe* (pans the kids on stage) I'd say for one night you can 'kind'a feel, what it feel's like to be a star, if that if anything should be a nice walk in *time,* should you live many'a'years (winks again, then zones out

180

before speaking) Now go home, all of you, and make sure to stay away from coughers, god knows I don't want none of you getting sick before the show

Danielle leaves rehearsal kissing Nelson step for step, apparently careless, without a worry in her mind

Storm Clouds appear, but her illuminating smile shines thru...

Until a voice cries out

Hermin-Yo Nel!
Nelson- Herm! Long time no see
Hermin- pardon me (speaking to Danielle, then turns to Nelson blankly) my cousin in Astoria told me that one of Taheem's friends is in for it
Nelson- what'dya mean (confused)
Hermin- there was another robbing
Nelson-what?
Hermin- yeah, and this time they beat him bad
Nelson-who?
Hermin- my cousin, Mario
Nelson-AGAIN
Hermin- yeah but this time they O'Dee'd on it (looking at Danielle)
Nelson- Danielle can you go order a slice for me (tipping nose at pizza shop) I'll be in a minute
Danielle- kay, but hurry up
Nelson- jus be a second (feeble attempt at a smile) promise (she goes gingerly)
Hermin- sorry didn't mean to bring the streets between you
Nelson- Would've found us anyway, at least this way I got a beat up on it

Hermin- well anyway, they might bring shit this time
Nelson- I'm used to that already, fuck'n Eastern European bottle party
Hermin- no (dense voice) most the 'bigbrothers carry
Nelson-Carry? (stunned)

Hermin- some of those guys are real crazy Nelson, it's no problem to tweek anybody
Nelson-even kids
Ermin- anybody (no joke) plus it's not just anybody, it's Mario's brother and if he doesn't do anything, it's going to make him look weak, and he can't have that in the kind of shit he's in
Nelson-whats'he a drug dealer
Hermin- no, but I think he's involved

And there the conversation ends. Danielle calls from Pizza place

Danielle- Nelson, your foods here! (Stares of venom to Hermin)
Nelson- Look Erm, call me and tell me when they coming, so I can warn Tah' and them
Hermin- that's the thing, I know you close to them, but I'm not, and Mario's my cousin, we family
Nelson- (Nelson has no wisdom for this and has not time to dwell) Yo we're friends and I know we can do something…
Hermin-Yeah right (harsh, disbelieving)
Danielle-EXCUSE ME!ARE YOU FINISHED!
Nelson- look I gotta go (running across the street)
Hermin-(reluctantly turns,echoes message walking away) try not to be around them too much, Lamott and them, and watch for kids that don't go here!
Nelson- I will
Hermin- you left an impression when you fought in December
Nelson- I only hit one kid
Hermin- you're posted!
Nelson- Yeah I guess (turns hard) later Erm
Hermin-bye

Nelson strolls over tranquilly, to ease her nerves

Danielle-what's going on?
Nelson-nothing, senseless bullshit
Danielle- I don't want you fighting
Nelson-(obvious) I don't want me fighting either

They sit on tenement building steps next to Sal's pizza

Danielle- you're doing so well right now (palms his hand) I can feel the streets leaving

Nelson- They were never in me to begin with Danny

Danielle- you're wrong Nelson, the Demons know you're kicking them out, and they're going to make an effort to stay

Nelson- (funny expression dawns his profile) girl, I'm not even going to answer that (tries to kiss her)

Danielle- (pushes him away) Stop it Listen! I saw you the other night with snakes over your legs

Nelson-snakes?

Danielle-bad dream

Quiet

Nelson- stop being a ghostbuster and come woman (grabs her) why you acting so crazy for, I told you I won't fight and I won't, promise

Danielle- You know (takes long breath before speaking again) your'Luck doesn'tcome without'price

Danielle glares silently for few seconds that seem like an eternity to Nelson

Nelson- whateva

Dannielle's face is seen gazing at Nelson, her eye sparkling crystal blue, as the scene fades out doing a twirl of black fade around her pupil, till only a circle of sapphire can be seen
(*SceneEnd)

(* Scene Int-) There the backdrop will unravel again to clouds mixed with clear blue skies. It's a windy day, as seen by Richie Conelly's blowing shirt. Seph, Glen and Cristian are walking towards the playground where can be seen many bodies surrounding the ballcourt. Glen comes forward as Seph reaches the hoop first and welcomes him

Seph- what up' Glen
Glen-THE SKY
Cris-where the bodysnatcher's?
Glen- them zombie nigga's ain't show up yet
Richie-Yo'sef my man!
Seph- RC'FiftyFour ("54" Two numbers always's on the back of Richie's jacket or sneakers) Where's Junebug?
Junebug- (popping in from behind) Well'well'well! The three stooge's!
Seph- (giving Junebug a dap) was wonder'n where you was, thought you got scared
Junebug- man, I ain't neva' scared
Cris- hope not
Glen- (looking sideways) why?
Cris- cause here they come

From the opposite field, the gang of drug dealers that beat them for "RIGHTS TO THE PARK" walk over, one of which, the tallest and heaviest of the group confronts JuneBug

Tyson-what up lil'man
Junebug- (head tilted away) what up Tice
Glen- yo, who you say'n little man too?
Tyson-fuck is't to'you (looking at JuneBug) this yo'baby nigga
JuneBug- (holding Glen back, grinning proudly) this my public relations advisor (speaking to Tyson) no'never'mind him, he jus doin' his job
Tyson- yea, his job bout to get his ass twisted up in this piece
Domingo-Yo'Tyson! We starting!
Tyson- (punches basketball out Glen's hands) Meet you on the court (stares at Junebug) nIGGER

Glen being held back by Junebug again

Glen- I'm gonna knock his teeth out
Junebug- yea, sure (comical look) how' bout you protect me after

we win this game

Glen- no doubt cousin

Seph- (running over) you guys ready for the rules

Cris- rules is they ain't no rules (tying his laces)

Seph-look we play'n till twenty one, switch at ten

Richie- we usually play to sixteen, what's the big deal with four extra buckets

Glen- five you mean (pokes Richies Jerzee, glowing a brilliant "54")

Richie-okayFIVE, MATHS'TURBATOR (Glen laughs) why two-one

Cris- I don't know, they want halfcourt outs

Seph-wow, they goin all NBA (muttering hard) vampires

One of the dealers comes over

Dealer- you ready to ROCK (points at ball)

Seph- (looks back at everyone on his side) we ready

Dealer- last time we met, we didn't get a chance to formally introduce ourselves, names Caesar by the way, and tha's Ricky (points at a short black man), tha's my' son Rambo (points to stocky teen) that's Domingo (points at pudgy man)

Glen- and let me guess (pointing at Tyson) that's Iron Mike (Richie cracks up)

Tyson- yeah especially to you (looking at Rich) HONKY

Richie- that was nice flush you had other game (sarcasm)

Tyson- yeah, too bad it wasn't on yo'mama

Junebug-lets go!

Court
is set
and
the
pieces
are all
in
place
for
game
to
begin
_____

Seph- you know if we lose, we gon'have a lot of explaining to
do (stares at parents watching their kids playing in the sandbox
behind the court)
Cris- well we might as well win then
Seph- (they slap hands) yea
Glen- (passing by Seph, speaking fast) you love birds ready to
serve them fools
Cris- no doubt

   It begins
   Dealers take the ball out on there own side, Rambo is
HANDLING the rock (ball), he see's his dad Caesar set a PICK
for him near the three point line, Rambo takes it then hands it
off to his dad rolling to the side for an open shot. Swish, the
ball goes right through

Caesar- Duece! (Rubs his sons head) and one ASSIST

   Glen comes over to take the ball out for the kitchen
boys, when Junebug suddenly interrupts

Junebug-let white'chocolate HANDLE it
Glen- I'll give it up at the half
Junebug-remember what happen'd las time (points to Cris)

   Glen does not look happy handing the ball to Cris,
and nudges June on the way down

   Cris brings it up, he looks off Seph who is open for a
second, but then thinks better of it knowing he can beat Rambo
OFF THE DRIBBLE, which he does going to the basket, when
Tyson comes over to pick him up (Defensive Breakdown) he has
to leave Rich, which he hopes Cris doesn't see

   But he does, and gives it up to Rich for the easy lay in

Richie-White chocolate (Slaps Cris on the ass) DROPPIN DIMES

1"Handle" A person who can dribble a basketball with great skill. A player who is hard to take a ball away from when bouncing it

2"Off the dribble" In basketball, when a player can get by a defender while dribbling the ball and create his own opportunity to shoot or pass the ball

3"Defensive Breakdown" Usually happens when a player gets by his man "Off the dribble" with the ball and it takes another man or two to stop his momentum to the hoop (score). When this happens other teammates are left open and the man "Handling" the ball can "Pass" the ball to his unguarded teammates for easy opportunities (score) *Other terms for a "Pass" that turns into points for other teammates are "Assist", "Droppin' Dimes", or " Nice Look"

4"Fast Break" Is a style of offense in basketball where a team, as soon as they get possession of the ball, run quickly down to the other side and try to score. It is usually used when a team has advantages in speed or stamina, hoping the other team can't keep up, wears down, or both

Rambo brings the ball up

Immediately Cris and Glen double team him and force him into a bad pass, which end's up in the hands of Seph who out jumps Ricky for it and quickly springs toward the hoop, laying it in

Tyson- Yo! (Seething at Rambo, calling Ricky over) can you handle this (rips ball out Rambo's grasp)
Ricky- yeah
Caesar-what's goin on?
Tyson- your son can't handle this (gives ball to Ricky) tell your son to play defense and not let that Cracka in the lane
Rambo- shit Tice, they double'd me
Caesar- shut up and get on that Whiteboy good!
Rambo-FUCK

Ricky take's the ball down getting hassle'd by Glen, when Tyson sets a PICK near halfcourt which level's Glen, and starts to run toward the hoop knocking over Richie at the foul line, Junebug tries to catch him but it's too late, Ricky lobb's the ball up for Tyson

Tyson catches it at the baseline, where he backs Seph down for an easy bank shot

Tyson- none these nigga's can guard me! (Running past Rich still dazed on the floor) specially you, HONKY
Junebug- yo chill wit that
Tyson- CHIN-CHIL-LA-NUTS

Caesar laughs

Caesar- these kids are soft out here
Richie- pull me (raises hand toward Junebug, who reaches down and pulls Rich off the floor)
Junebug- you want me to get him (staring at Tyson)
Richie- help out when they I-so (Isolation) but man on man, he'd just shoot over you (see's little ones on the sideline watching the game) I'll figure something out, don't worry

Rich hands the ball off to Cris and they run downcourt, Junebug see's Tyson at the baseline and rams his shoulder into him trying to create space, as Cris bounces the ball into the middle

Tyson- (smiling) switch!

Tyson guard's Junebug and Domingo covers Rich
Tyson hoping that Junebug forces a bad shot out of anger, is took off guard when he passes it over Domingo's head to a much taller Richie, who easily shoot's over the shorter defender

Rich- (to June) nice look
Junebug- (tapping his head) these dudes ain't too smart

188

The game goes on for more then an hour before tides start turning against Junebug and company

A hard foul by Tyson lands Glen out of bounds, grimacing in pain

Nelson comes out nowhere helps him up

Glen- fuck you come from (puzzled)
Nelson- why Merry Christmas to you too

Richie run's over to haul Seph and Glen back on court

Glen- thanks Michael Microsoft (messing up Nelson's hair)
Richie- what up Nelly'Nel (looks him off) HurryU, these dudes don't hear timeout, you too Glen, get back-get back!
Nelson- whoa, this looks like its'bout to get intresting
Seph- (running back on court) yeah, enjoy pussy
Nelson- (rooting for his friend) PLEASE WIN THIS TIME

Everyone is now on court, as one of the dealers makes a statement

Tyson-What's count?
Richie-fifteen twelve (15-12)
Tyson- now I know we got more than that, I damn near six points my 'damn self
Richie- sixteen twelve (16-12)
Caesar- we ain't got all day what's count
Tyson- TEN
 Richie- TWELVE
Tyson- ten bread crumb
Richie- twelve monkey

Tyson raises a fist up to Rich but Caesar moves between, dividing them

Caesar-look the counts fifteen eleven, that good wit you (15-11)
Glen- how we go down point
Junebug-(grabbing his lil cousin) yeah, fifteen eleven (15-11)
we hold rock
Caesar- TWENTY ONE STRAIGHT
                                    (First Team to 21 wins)
Junebug- no win by two? (As in tennis, must win by more then
one point *i.e: If the score is 20-20 then 22 becomes the winning
point. But Caesar states that it is 21 STRAIGHT, meaning no
matter WHAT, the team that gets to 21 points first, wins)
Caesar-don't have time'playa
Junebug-fine (throws ball to Caesar) CHECK

The game resumes, with the kitchen boys letting the
other team score one more bucket (point), before coming back
in a whirlish dirlish kind of motion, using their youth as an
advantage and speeding the tempo of the game with full court
press, leading to steals and havoc, while on offense executing
the FAST BREAK, distributing the rock (passing) pushing the
ball upcourt as fast their feet can carry them, leaving the
dealer's with hands on knees, desperate for air

By the time the come back is complete, the kitchen
boys are up nineteen to seventeen (19-17) two points away

Caesar- Time out! (Puts knee on floor, unable to breathe)
Stop play!

Caesar groups his team up, into team huddle while pouring
bottled water over his head. The others look drained too, except
for Tyson, he just looks mad as HELL

Rambo-what's the deal
Caesar- SON! (Rambo, is Caesar the Crack dealers son) you see
that kid there (points to Junebug)
Rambo- yeah (Rambo see's Tyson coming and turns from his
dad, focusing now on Tyson's biceps)
Tyson-what's goin on?
Caesar- (grabs Rambo by neck) LISTENS, next time he goes up

Rambo- for a shot

Caesar- for a shot, for board, anything, just make sure when he go up, you slide your foot under, so he land on top your laces

Rambo- DAD, ain't that gonna roll his ankle

Caesar- EXACTLY, like THIS (Caesar bends his wrist back) make sure he turns it

Rambo- (reluctantly, half hearted voice) yea, alright

Caesar- GO (pushes him) and don't be a PUSSY bout'it!

Junebug rechecks the ball, youngsters get back on Defense

Junebug- (smiling) YO, what's that movie where them old folks find that pool and start BREAKDANCIN' AND SHIT, oh yeah COCOON, YO' COCOON!! COMEOUT' COCOON!! BREAK DANCE' ON THIS (grabs his genetalia) TOP'ROCK BODY'ROCK TO THIS COCOON!!

Caesar- (whispering, unhearable) check ball

Junebug- OH! The strong silent type, I like that

Caesar- CHECK!

Caesar gets the ball, and see's Tyson push off Richie to create space, he does. Caesar passes to Tyson, Tyson turns and shoots missing badly off the glass, it bounds toward Rambo who is underneath the hoop, Rambo catches and tries to put it back, when out of nowhere Junebug fly's and punches it so far that it ends up near the halfcourt line, where Cristian is there to grab it and break to the basket for an easy bucket. Cristian pumps his fist and hollers

Cris- Point game PRICKS (one point away from win)

But when he turns, he see's Seph bent over someone on the pavement

Cris- (running up) what happen?

Seph- I don't know, but help him

Glen- (shaking) where you hurt cousin

Junebug- (in pain) think I rolled my shit   191

Rich- (running in with snow cone a toddler gave him on the side, rainbow colored) here put this on

Glen-Yo' Rich what happened?

Rich- this dude right here (pointing to Rambo) slid his kicks under June when he was comin' down

Caesar- (laughing) ridiculous

Rich- you fella's can't win a fair one so you have to resort to this garbage to get a W (takes an angry step). SELL'N CRACK while kid's is runn'n around!

Tyson- (looks at Junebug) better calm your man down right there before he catches it

Rich- without a gun (killer grin) you'd be out your mind

Tyson- no gun, let's do it (as he walks toward Rich, Caesar stops him with a smile)

Caesar- look I'm sorry 'bout your friend here, but without a fifth you gon' have to forfeit

Glen- Junebug?

Junebug- Seph, get off me (he tries to walk but is obvious that the ankle cannot hold his weight)

Rich- we just need one point

Junebug- I'd slow ya'll down

Rich- you could just hang back and cherry pick, we bound to catch a board without'cha and beam one back

Junebug- nah, they just hang nigga back here wit me, SHIT! Ain't there anyone on the side that can take my spot!

Rich look's around and sees little one's too small, along with parents, whom are silent.

From the corner of his eye he glimpses Seph pulling a short Asian boy

Seph- hurry up, HURRY (dragging Nelson)

Nelson- Seph this ain't my GAME! I'm not gonna be able to do nutt'n

Seph- YO' RICH, THIS NIGGA SAY HE WANNA PLAY

Glen- Jack of all trades huh, dance'n, ball'n, what next, fried rice

The dealers see him and begin to smirk and cackle. Rich see's this and cut's in

Rich-Nelson, you play'n?
Nelson- (silent) uh...
Seph- yeah he play'n
Rich- you know we play'n ZONE right
Nelson-zone?
Rich- ZONE!! as in (grabbing him over to the left side of the foul shot) anybody that come here you get in front of
Seph- oh stop acting nigga, you know what zone is (pushing Nelson to his spot)
Cris- I thought we was play'n man on
Rich- we WAS, but without June we're too small (waits for Junebug to safely limp off) look's like we're gonna have to LIVE AND DIE with this zone (yell's to team) READY!!

One by one they give Rich the thumbs up to check ball, and in an instant, play resumes

Tyson- we gonna score four straight right now (he looks over at Caesar) POST! POST! POST, CAESAR GIVE IT TO ME, KILL THE WANG!! (we all know who the "WANG" is)

Nelson is targeted by the opposing team to be the weak link , easy to get by, which draws Cristian and Seph out the middle to guard the man he let thru. Result: Middle of the paint is wide open for Tyson to be one on one with Rich, who is easily POSTED on

Tyson scores three times in a row... Making the game tied at twenty *20

Rich-Hold Rock!

Rich calls timeout and devices plan

Rich- look (grabs Nelson close to him) if we don't score here, next time on defense, I want you to break ZONE
Cris- (stunned) break the *zone*?
Seph- that's gonna leave the three wide open!

Rich- SHH! (Turns to see their not in earshot) we gonna have to risk that, cause Yoshi here is let'n'em'n too easy
Seph- what we do after we break it, I don't know Rich everybody's gonna be left WIDE OPEN?

Rich- they're open already, the cat's out the bag (stares at Nelson)
Cris- (screams to Nelson) DAMN MAN DO SOMETHING!!
Rich- CRIS, STOP! (Cris walks away from the huddle)
Nelson, as soon as they get by you, I want you to run right under their big man (Tyson) and strip the ball, while he's posting me
Glen- Rich you buggin'
Seph- I'm wit Glen on this one, down the Blocks've been brutal all'day (best friend look) Nels'would'beCRUSHED
Rich- trust me it's gonna work, he ignores this kid like he don't EXIST, we can use that (face to face) now you're only gonna have one shot at this, so wait til'he turns that big shoulder of his before taking a swipe at it. (Nelson looks at the kids glaring on the sideline) Yoshi! (pushes his head) noodles'straight!
Nelson-yea
Rich-remember, ONE SHOT

They walk back to the line greeted by cheers from the crowd, especially Junebug. The crowd seems to know what the boys are actually playing for, thanks to an injured player from the neighborhood
Junebug- Give'em'Hell fiftyfour!

Rich glances to the sideline and see's a roaring crowd, catching a glimpse of his friend barely able to stand, pumping his fist toward them, quickly looking down after a slight smile, then patting Nelson on the back giving him a wink of Celtic Luck
Rich- CHECK!!!

Cristian gets the ball looking off Glen, then passes to Seph. Seph waits for a SCREEN by Glen pretending to take it, when suddenly breaks and rolls to the basket, floating the ball up for a shot. It's blocked, glancing off Cristian's ear out of bounds

Tyson- we want the rock on the otherside... I hope you happy wit'yourselves (spiteful) now all them can clap on the PIPE
Cris- game ain't over yet
Tyson-YOU STIL'YAPPIN, FACE PUNCHED, STIL'YAPP'N, (laughing) *whiteboys'man*

     Nelson gets in place for collapsing ZONE defense, going over what Rich told him in his mind. He goes over it but can't see it clearly. At that juncture of thought a boy from the jungle gym ahead of the court, falls from a swing and is helped up by a girl with pig'tails', she starts to yell for no reason
     ~Nelson is hypnotized by the girls voice

Tyson- CHECK HONKEY!!

     Ball checks into Tyson's hands, he immediately hands the ball over to Caesar and runs toward the hoop where he's met by Rich. Richie is losing ground to Tyson fast, Nelson breaks ZONE DEFENSE when Caesar lobs it in, running toward the two as planned, the balls already with Tyson, he dips his shoulder into Richard creating space, he instantly jumps over Rich for the slam, he dunks and holds the rim... But nothing goes in, thee'ball is missing

     Crowd screams

     Tyson while hanging on the hoop can see bodies flying to the otherside
     Cristian crosses over Domingo leaving him still as a parking meter.

     In a flash Rich cuts to the basket with only Caesar to beat, Cristian swings him the ASSIST. Caesar see's this and knowing he's to slow to catch Rich sticks a foot out to trip the blazing teen

It never makes it

Caesar fanatically trying to tangle up Rich never see's Seph at the three line, set for a PICK that Caesar crashes into "like a drunk driver 'drive'n, and there ain't no survive'n"

Suddenly Rich has a clearing

Junebug- (chanting with the crowd) FLY'IRISH FLY!!

Rich see's clear path to the promiseland, but then notices a large figure CRASHING toward the basket

It's Tyson

They're both blazing to the hole, screams are coming from the sideline. it seems the whole neighborhood has come

Tyson- don't try it cornflake

Tyson- I'M BLACK, I'M FIRST!!

Richie closes his eyes and goes all in

They take flight

In slowest motion both ascend high, growing closer

Tyson is above Rich at their peak, but a gush of wind blows past everyone on the field and lifts Rich above Tyson
        A man's hand is seen throwing a thumbs'up sign, then mumbling few words

St. Patrick- O'those smile'n eyes'

BOOM! A ball Jams in over Tyson, and the crowd Implodes, as Rich SLAM DUNKS one for the ages.

Almost at once the dope peddlers begin leaving the field, slowly walking toward the gates of "Clinton De'Witt". Their sagging shoulders and humble silence as the last remembrance of what they really were

Perpendicular to them is Glen, Cristian, Junebug all being lifted by the crazed mob. Seph is shaking hands with a group of parents while being introduced to thier kids, adding his shiny whites to dozens of other teeth, still growing in.

Nelson unnoticed, begins to walk offcourt, when out of nowhere a voice turns him

Rich- I think you left something
Nelson- (confused) hi
Rich- say this ball isn't yours is it
Nelson- I didn't bring a ball down
Rich- yea you did (giving it to him) you brought this (ball) down and the whole ROCK at the same time (crunching a crack vile with his heel)
Nelson- man, I'm sorry I had all them guy's runn'n through like that
Rich- Hey, ya came through when it counted, that's all I sees' (greenery) you know these trees here grown dark since these demons been selling here, maybe they won't look so depress'n after alls'this shit been cleaned out
St. Patrick- The sound of them young ones should bring them back in no time (Staring at children, now re-taking the field)
Rich-Nelson, you know that guy?
Nelson- no (says this queerly) looks familiar tho'
Rich- was'jus bout to say that (The Saint walks away, as Rich and Nelson look upon him)

~View starts to lift, summer sprinklers are passed, then park benches and winter leaves blown through are cleared, the ballpark beyond the fence, then warehouses and tenements of the Kitchen are passed, fading out the New York skyline.

Finally the scene grows toward the blue sky, till nothing can be seen but the sun, and there the view stays, until the light of the fiery ball blinds the whole spectrum, fading into camera light and onto Oxford's stage for Nelson's last rehearsal

Nelson is twirling his wooden Oscar in the air without care in the world, when out of nowhere a hand snatches it

Abdul-(Catching wooden Oscar, placing it carefully on his chair) Make sure mine got mushrooms on it
Michael- Make mine wit'extra cheese
LaTanya- (runs over) somebody goin'out for pizza
Farooz- (coming down from stage) delivery boy, Sushi boy
Nelson- ok that's it, no more orders
Farooz- he said orders (giggling)
Nelson- Tanya what you want
LaTanya-jussum'them garlic twists
Abdul- no wonder why your breath stank
LaTanya-shut up shortee
Nelson- Farooz, anything
Farooz- just a large fruit punch

They gather the money up and let Nelson know he can keep the extra

Farooz- you know like a tip, delivery tip
Nelson- (flipping the bird) Farooz your punch might be tangy'er then usual if you don't stop wit'the wise cracks (hacks up spit sound)
Farooz- ungh, that's nasty

Nelson walks up the ramp and out the auditorium

Danielle- (Just coming out the bathroom notices him leaving) wheres' he going?
Farooz-The Cheese spot (blasé')

*Nelson goes in Sal's pizza shop and makes his order, the camera flashes and moneys exchanged, with another flash where the food and Farooz's large punch is being handed to Nelson, with a nice pat on the shoulder from the oven mitt guy. When Nelson walks out everything comes in segments, as time is jammed in his relevance

1$^{st\text{-}blink}$ – A teen in a hooded sweater runs up and knocks food out Nelson's hand
2$^{nd\text{-}blink}$ – He takes swing at Nelson with a shiny object, blood sprays out
3$^{rd\text{-}blink}$ – The attacker stops and looks at the blood, unbeknownst that his hoody has fallen revealing an Hispanic male
4th blink$^{th\text{-}blink}$– Nelson punches the attacker in the face
5$^{th\text{-}blink}$-Attacker drops to the floor unconscious, oven mitt guy from Sal's pizza runs out to see what's happening, then ducks down hearing loud shots fired
6$^{th\text{-}blink}$- Nelson turns and see's a flying body ram right into him, knocking him back to sit on tenement steps next to the pizzeria. Nelson lays there with person who rushed him
7$^{th\text{-}blink}$- A car is heard skidding off with feint sounds of sirens coming from distance
8$^{th\text{-}blink\text{-}}$ Italian guy picks up VHS tape which falls from Chez'co's pocket, who is still out cold   ←p*36,69
9$^{th\text{-}blink\text{-}}$A girl looks up from Nelson's lap and caresses his hair

Nelson-Ana!
Ana- (blood is pooling on her white tee) *hi*
Nelson- Dee'dee!
Ana- need to tell you something (coughing)
Nelson- (Screaming to pedestrians) SOMEBODY'CALL AN AMBULANCE!
Ana- I feel cold, can you hold me
Nelson- Cold?
Ana- can't feel my legs, I think I been… (Senses something and holds him tight) I'm sorry 'bout'the other day I didn't mean to...

Nelson- (blood is spilling on the pavement) DIANA!
Ana- sleepy
Nelson- (panic) don't sleep, UP, CAN YOU STAND

Quiet sets in

Ana- been while since we… I miss (she begins to shake, and slur her speech) I miss you

Nelson kisses her and there she fades

Blue and Red lights twirl the Oxford entrance, as sirens along with walkie talkies pierce the atmosphere

*Nelson's mind, hears voices

- "I often wonder…"
- "Wonder what?"
- "Why you never ask me out"
- "Is my boat unsinkable?"
- "I saw snakes…"
- "Ol' Scratch, saw money to be made"
- "Luck doesn't come without price (echo)… a price"

All in the show is now rushed out to the street, being held back by police lines

Mr. Bridge- (speaking to cop whose stick is poking him) LOOK I KNOW WHAT BACKUP MEANS OK, but see that child (fingers Nelson laid over Ana) that's one of mine officer!

Detective jargon oils in
"There's three caps here captain, still' hot, and some burnt rubber on that stripe" another voice grinds through "Must've been drive by"

Nelson- (closes Ana's eyelids, kissing her forehead gently, he sheds a tear) goodnight princess

Flash of white blinds the whole spectrum, then at its brightest pinnacle begins to fade, as the view drops toward New Jersey Freeways across the river, to the streets of Manhattan's Westside, then finally to Nelson's roof, where he's standing, alone

*   *   *

@ }—'--,-------------- 12

THERE'S A DOG LOST IN THE WOODS

Int- Seph's back is seen walking toward Nelson, they're both facing away

Seph- (kicking dirt on the ground) what up family
Nelson-(deaf)
Seph- they asked about you at the wake, the funerals this Wednesday
Nelson-(deaf)
Seph- (places a card on the rooftop fence) thought you might hang on to this
Nelson-(deaf)
Seph- you know (buttoning his jacket) the mailbox in the lobby was flooded from a busted pipe Sunday and they had Joel wring'n out all the letters, he looked like he was make'n chicken quisadilla's (forced chuckle)
Nelson-(deaf)
Seph- so uh, wow, windy up here
Nelson-(deaf)

Seph see's he's not going to get anything out of him and starts backing away

Seph- Whoa, (card almost blows away from the wind) better put this here where you can see it (sighs) anyway, Joel ran into an envelope with your name on it (pulls it out) says Les'Guardants (waits for reaction)
Nelson- (nothing)
Seph- didn't know you was try'n out to get in there

Nelson-(deaf)

Seph-(waits)

Seph- (pats him on the back and walks off speaking) well'uh (long pause) good luck

Nelson-Thanks

Seph- (stops dead in his tracks and turns again)

Undecisevely Seph stands there for a moment

After doing a few walk toward roof door and couple steps back to Nelson whip lashes, he decides at the very end, when his hand is touching the staircase door, to just leave

The card still on the fence, where the wind has picked up has a birthdate of Diana Mela. Nelson still looking toward a fading sky never sees it, when a swift wind blows it away

Seph in the elevator waits for the door to open, when he gets out the lobby Cristian walks in almost kissing him

Seph- Yo, that was close

Cris- (wiping his lips) I'm for equal opportunity, but that's push'n it

Uncomfortable moment

Cris- he's up there? (taking a step toward the elevator when he feels Seph's hold)

Seph- just let him be

Cris- you don't think it's a funny time for him to be on the roof, A-lone

Seph- you know he ain't that soft nigga

Cris- hey, hey, hey

Seph-(sharply) HEY what?

Cris- he been zombied out for like five fuck'n days is WHAT

Seph- you'd be too

Cris- not if my BOYS come around and snap me out

Seph- come on man what the fuck you know
Cris- (about to react, but then goes another way) can I say
sumthin judge (raises hand playfully)
Seph- what
Cris- I just got off the R train and saw something very
interesting I think
Seph-and?
Cris- mind if I show you
Seph- tell me here
Cris- you don't trust me

      Seph stands there looking at Cristian irritated when he
starts walking out

Cris- (jokingly, selling it by waving his arms) come on lets go,
stop bein' a bitch (Cris smiles at Seph who is reluctantly walking)

      They pace toward the lobby entrance

Seph- hope you ain't plann'n on pushing me on them tracks
Cris- Stop bein an idiot
Seph- good, cause I wouldn't be the *only* one on that third rail
Cris- Guess you want me to be the first whiteboy wit' natural curls
Seph- you stupid

      Cristian, Seph out building.
~Scene fades

      Int- Trains can be heard screeching to a halt, then rumbling
out, as the two boys walk down steps of the R platform of 57th
street

      Both walk to the downtown side

Seph- how far we… (puts hand over his mouth) fucks that smell!

Cris- how many times we seen that bum (points to a homeless man sporting a tank top, no jacket, blowing steam out his nostrils into Febuary31st air)

Seph- I know he freez'n

Bum catches eye contact with them and smiles

Cris- we been hang'n out since way back, and everytime we been here, it's the same old stink from the same old bastard, say'n the same ol'shit, over and over

Seph- so

Cris- so he's stuck (looks at the bum) don't you THINK

Seph- move'n jus fine to me

Cris- you know what I'm say'n

Seph- what, you think nel's gonna be like that

Seph watches bum pee in his pants and starts to giggle

Cris- something funny (dead serious)

Seph- come on man, you talk'n nonsense yo

Cris- maybe, but look at it this way, I bet that guy was just two or three moments away from bein doctor or football player'somebody, when…

Seph- when what, CRACK got in the way

Cris- circumstances can lead to that

Seph- circumstance ha! Five dolla word for given up

Cris- MAY'BEE he wouldn't have gave up if he had some help

Boys are now silent as a train whistles by blowing off newspapers covering the homeless man, one of the papers blown reads "DRAMACIDE" with a photo of Nelson holding Ana's head covered in blood. A roach crosses the bums path and he raises a boot letting it pass under, where it is then come down, slowly crushed. He lay's back down and spins a cracked model of globe on its axis, humming Nat Cole's standard "Fly me to the moon"

Seph- I think you're blow'n this out context
Cris- what you say to him when you were up there
Seph- just try'n get Nel to open up, gave him the wake card and letter they sent from that performing arts school right across from M.L.K
Cris- Nelson got a letter from Les'Guardants?
Seph- yea, why
Cris- my girl Kara goes there, she tunes the robot piano it's probably an audition invitation
Seph- exactly, so I told him good luck and went on my way
Cris- she helps with the set up for those auditions. She can tell me when Nel is up
Seph- hol up (eyebrows raised) what for?
Cris- make it like this (puts hand on Seph's shoulder pointing him to the Hobo) if we don't hear nutt'n from him all the way to the eve of this tryout (begins to squeeze Seph's shoulder) we're gonna DRAG him out

Seph slaps Cristian's hand off disapprovingly, but after hearing the bum wail out an ungodly squeal and see him undress his pants in public, realizes Cris has a point

Seph- ok, find out
Cris- ok

Another train passes where compartment lights in most of the cars are flashing, last of these cars blinks lights on and off so rapid that the scene becomes blurred, after a few seconds the blinking slows down and Mr. Bridge can be seen speaking to members of the show, inside class

Int- Mr. Bridge surveys every child in his room, and waits patient for opportune time to speak

Bella- (speaking to Raven) guess the shows over (gets nasty stare from Danielle)

Mr. Bridge- I'm afraid our production has been halted, for reasons you're all too familiar with

Bella- (loud) what a waste

Mr. Bridge- (coughing over Bella, and catching eye contact with most of the cast) well if anyone has a word, now's the time

Bella- (whispering to Raven) pop, pop, pop

Danielle- (tosses her bag nearly hitting Bella in the head, and jumps to her feet) MOUTH BITCH!

LaTanya-(stands fast) YEAH! FUCK HER UP DANNY, I GOT YOU (stares at Raven)

Mr. Bridge-SIT' DOWN LATANYA

LaTanya- hate jealous bitches I swear (fixing her hair)

Mr. Bridge- QUIET AND PEACE

Bella- (Ignoring whole episode, still jawing) thought Danielle was white

Raven- *wuzz'* is the correct word

Bella- I think I liked her better then

Danielle sits down banging her chair

Abdul stands Up

Abdul- Mr. B is there any way we can go on with the show with me and Michael filling in Nels spots

Mr. Bridge- we would have to find another student to learn your parts and Michaels to replace

Michael- I know some people who would be down to come in for me and Abdul, they "House", "BodyRock", all that

Mr. Bridge- the stage has a tight schedule for Spring and unless your friends can learn the routines in no less then a week and perform them confidently, I'm afraid the show is cancelled

Abdul- they can remember most of it

Mr. Bridge- I hold myself to excellence, so a brush job is no option Abdul

Michael- can we cut some of the show

Mr. Bridge- absolutely not, what an insane thing to say

Michael- I know it sounds bad but at least we can perform some of it, instead of letting it all go

Mr. Bridge- The show must go on, but we are going to wait for a replacement. The only option is to postpone the event till summer. June is the next available date, of course by that time the yearbooks would be in complete jeopardy, for those of you who don't know, the tickets sold for this concert was suppose to go to your yearbooks. Looks like for graduating students the yearbooks will have to be mailed during your break   *←P.70

The cast looks lost for words

Raven- (to Bella) talk'bout putting all your eggs in one basket

Mr. Bridge- we lost a cornerstone of the show and there's no possible way around it, I'm sorry but until further notice... the play is cancelled

Cast shuffles out, quietly grabbing their coats

LaTanya and Michael come over to Dannielle

LaTanya- they'll be better days girl

Michael- yea danny, keep ya head up

Dannielle- thanks Mike (gets a rose from Michael and tea box from LaTanya) thanks Tanya (Farooz comes over as LaTanya walks away)

Farooz-hey danny

Danielle- hey rooz

Mr. Bridge is seen waving to Danielle

Mr.Bridge- Danielle

She turns and tells Farooz to go

Mr. Bridge- one word please

Danielle- (walks over to his desk) sorry' bout before

Mr. Bridge- don't be

Danielle- you're not mad?

Mr. Bridge- why, because someone was walking all over your face and you decided to bite a foot off

Danielle- you heard her?

Mr. Bridge- I'm not deaf, and I see all the ruthless things her and Raven do during rehearsal to you guys

Danielle- (surprised) well, (pause) if you see it why do you let her...

Mr. Bridge- your boyfriend has a gift but tis'not enough, and we'll just leave it at that

Danielle- Nelson

Mr. Bridge- he needs to learn a few things before he goes flying off toward the stars (pulls out a wooden Oscar from his pocket, then looks at her sternly) have you heard from him?

Danielle- not for few days no, but that's natural for what just happened isn't it

Mr. Bridge- you need to go to him

Danielle- I can't right now, I wouldn't know how he would react (she begins to weep) that girl who died, I just found out today she was... (wipes her eyes) she may not known I was with him all this time

Mr. Bridge- (takes her hand and passes her the wooden statue of Oscar) she died so he could live. He's not LIVING right now, if you want to clean the slate then get him to be the way he was

Danielle- what is this? (looking at statue)

Mr. Bridge- It's something that will remind him that where the rain's hard, LIGHTNING ALSO STRIKE

Danielle- I don't understand

Mr. Bridge- it's an inside thing (winks)

Danielle-(chuckling through tears) should I apologize

Mr. Bridge- no (gets her up firmly) just give him that (points at hand holding wooden Oscar) for me (kisses her on the forehead and squeezes extra tight) now go WAKE HIS ASS UP

Danielle- (gleaming smile) yes Mr. B
Mr. Bridge- GO!   _End scene

@ }—'--,-------------
13

THOR STRIKES THE ANVIL

Int- Les'Guardant High. A large table is placed in what seems to be a ballet center with mirrors and banisters lining the walls. Four teachers sitting behind the table watch a young boy come in being met by teachers aid, given a script

Within the hallway outside the ballet studio is a line of teens as far as the eye can see, waiting for their turn, one of which is Nelson

Outside eating bagel talking to Seph in front of the entrance is Cristian

Seph- yo I can't believe you got me up this early on a Sunday, just to hogtie a nigga out his build'n and pull him to this boo'zhee shit
Cris- (tearing half a bagel for Seph and hands him a cup of coffee) just munch on this you fuck'n jungle bunny
Seph- you wish you were

A garbage truck with the words "Change Trash Co." rolls by

Cris- where the hell that football Al-head been, haven't seen him in eons
Seph- probly'bleaching his skin, who knows

Steam pours out both faces in the bitter cold

Cris- Christ it's early (drinks coffee down at once)
Seph- fuck'n Neandrathals I swear (tastes his coffee) you suppose to sip the cafe'
Cris- I don't do fag style

Seph- whatever (looking at his watch) how long this shit gonna take

Cris- as long as it takes. (they stare at each other) wanna go to that library right there (points across the street)

Seph- (stamping his foot) damn, that's a library? Must be some spoiled brats up here to be have'n elevator libraries

Cris- well it sure beats the piece'a shit libraries we got in the Kitchen

Seph- (tossing his bagel wrapper in garbage) you could say that again (gives a pound to Cristian, then crosses over) whats' he doing again?

~Scene flips to inside the audition

Int- Nelson is getting a short script from a young girl smiling bright

Cris's girl- break legs!

Trial begins. After few moments of Nelson reading from the pages he is stopped by one of the board members

Seated lady 1- that was very fluid (she raises her spectacles and begins reading his record)

Seated male 1- young man what program did you undergo?

Seated lady 1- (looks up from her papers) he's never been in a program

Seated male 2- astonishing (looks at seated lady2 then back to Nelson) have you taken private classes prior in your thespedic history

Seated lady 1- he's never had any formal training and it seems his academics are not up to par, at least not for this venue

Seated lady 2- well that can be changed, LesGuardant has overlooked GPA grades solely on talent merit before

Seated lady 1- his attendance is also at question, says here he's been late or absent one third of the time in his institution

Seated male 1- why, that (longest IS you ever heard) *is* alarming (looking at Nelson) what keeps you from being on time son

Nelson- (silent)

Seated male 1- well (waiting for him to speak)

Nelson-(silent)

Seated lady 1- you was asked about your punctuality young man (nelson is still silent) are you mocking us boy

Seated lady 2- GOODNESS, this is the child that was involved with that shooting just a week ago

The council immediately goes into a huddle and whisper frantically with most of the loud gestures coming from **Seated lady 2**. "Let's just see what he has before tossing him out!"

Seatedlady1- FINE

Children in the hall begin to peer in, curious about the grunts coming from within. Cris's girl closes the door

Seated male 2- are you ready lad (heavy English accent)

Nelson- (silent)

Seatedmale2- commence

Nelson- (stares at the Brit then cautiously looks at his reflection in the mirror)

Seated lady 1- Speak young man!

Seated lady 2- put a cork in it scroogee (turns back at Nelson who is now seated at the piano) go ahead sweetee

Closeseyes
TakesDeep
breath
Begins

Visions of adolescence begin to flood Nelson's mind as he plays

Vision one: Alec, Seph and Nelson, laying on top his

Roof watching clouds shoot across the sky. Seph puts his hand out catches a firefly cupping it, then passes it to Nelson where it lights up in his hand, flying off into darkness. Utter black darkness.

Vision two: Light from the bug tinkles again and it's now Cris in his kitchen with Nelson passing him a spatchler, showing him how to turn sunnyside eggs over to match hash browns already on his plate. Shadow, Cristian's cat passes by the bacons dripping on paper towels near the stove, taking a whiff as he passes. Nelson says "What purpose does it serve to teach me this" Cris retorts " This has nothing to do with you mate, I'm just showing you what I'm be making some tight cookie girl after I loosen her up in the morning" Nelson retorts "my mother must eat Mickey'D's breakfast" Nelson laughs at Cristians confusion but is cut short with Cris stating "You might want to take those out" points his fork to Nelson's eggs overcooking in the pan. The lightbug flys thru the kitchen but none see it, except for Shadow who paws at it but to no avail, as it passes around the cat and out the window. Nelson looks out the window right when the light fades but only see's Shadow quietly staring out, he faces the window and there see's his face reflect through the looking glass, where he is walking along a street late night. He goes into store stealing but is caught and shoved out by the cashier, who tosses him out hard, landing face first on a steel sewer cap. He kicks a garbage can into the gutter and after a moment, runs off, unknowing he was being watched by someone, a girl. The girl on the corner watches the streets as the firebug lands on her shoulder, revealing her face an instant like a turned page, then dowsed out, with Nelson walking off into a sunset, where leaves are falling.

Vision three: Richie Connelly is holding a pipe in his hands surrounded by hooligans. "You want this kid's radio!" Nelson is holding onto a boombox in the back of a handball court, with Rich fencing a gang of kids ready to attack "Nelson give me the BOX" Rich takes the radio knowing he can't stop everyone and decides to smash it on the floor, exploding metal, and a cassette which squirts out.

216

"Now it's everybody's BOX!!" Nelson nods a good yes and joins Rich to fight, when Junebug suddenly shows up with some neighborhood boys, that make the others run for their lives. The firebug flys through all the running thugs and twirls around the bark of a tree going into it. When it lights up again its' back where it started, on top Nelson's roof, this time it's night and stars are shooting across the sky. Nelson on his back with Seph, watches the shower illuminate the Universe around them, when without warning the roof door pops open catching Nelson's eye. When Nelson looks back, he sees his friends are gone but light from the firebug remains brilliant. The firebug flies in his palm and embers up a last time before the roof door slowly closes, awaking him along the last notes of a soft Piano

When Nelson awakes from playing, a red clover trickles down his left side, past an emotionless face.

Judges go into huddle, whispering even more aggressively this time
Most of it can be heard

Seated lady1- THIS WAS AN ACTING AUDITION YOUNG RAT (quickly corrects herself) YOUNG MAN, ACTING! NOT EBONY BANGING
Seated lady 2- That was more then ebony banging Eva, just on that alone he could qualify for a classical music course here
Eva- but today is not that day Jezebel, today is a try for Thespians!
Seated male 1- I don't want to choose sides (more towards Eva) but she is right, today is a tryout for acting, not music
Nelson- but I was acting

Nelson waves his fingers over the keys of the piano from end to end, and is silent all the way down

Seated male 1- (stands up) what's THIS... a joke?

Cris's girl takes radio out from inside the piano and hands it to Nelson, where he ejects a cassette

Eva- (face of death at Cris's girl) KARA, GO STAND NEXT TO THAT DOOR AND DO NOTHING ELSE TILL I SPEAK WITH YOU
Kara- yes mam (walks toward the door, slightly looking at Nelson on her way past, whispering) it was worth it (then winking with a grin) you're in

Teachers huddle for last and final time, then turn to Nelson for his verdict. Doors of the audition hall are plastered with ears, listening for judgement

Eva- I know his talent is undeniable, but he's so, so, unorthodox
Jezebel- UNORTHODOX! Now just exactly whats' that suppose to mean
Eva- shall I get a dictionary
Jezebel- this is OUTRAGEOUS
Seated male 1- sure the child has certain qualities Jezebel, but he's a liability, being involved in gang activity and all
Jezebel- gang activity Bill, (ludicrously) like Don Corleone
Bill- wasn't it YOU who said he was involved in a shooting
Eva- (sharply) abomination

The Brit speaks

Seated male 2- son (looks at the council then back to Nelson) you definitely have feel for this sort (Eva sucks her teeth) I've been in the game long enough to separate a true bard from the phonies, to dud and bomb, front-line center. But with all the violence in schools this year, and being right with preserving the integrity of being one of the only schools in New York with a clean Bill of health, from fighting and sexual charges, I can't see a place for you here lad. You'll find another institution that can nurture your raw ability I'm sure, but for this school, (looks at Jezebel) there's no place to fitted. (looks back at Nelson) I truly am sorry

A long second passes

Nelson- what'a'ya sorry for, it wasn't my idea to come here (grabs his coat passing Kara without saying a word)

Kara's clearly vexed at the outcome and calls in the next runner up stiffly

Kara- NEXT!

~Exit
Scene

Int- Snow begins to fall when Nelson steps out Les'Guardants, he begins to walk when…

Danielle- Hey sport!

Nelson is not moved one bit, and is looking with eyes which seem frozen

Danielle- aren't you going to say anything
Nelson-why you here
Danielle-the shows been rescheduled
Nelson- was it your idea for me to get man handled today and dragged the fuck out here
Danielle-what?
Nelson-nothing, where's Cris and Seph
Danielle- I saw them and asked if I could have a moment… (takes step) They left
Nelson- look have to go
Danielle- wait, what' bout the show

Nelson-what'bout it
Danielle- you're in most of the key parts
Nelson- just find somebody else
Danielle- you' know there's nobody Nelson
Nelson- sure there is, just get a dance'nigger

Racial remark hits her

Danielle- You know the dimension you add to the show,
you know it's more then just moves
Nelson- well, everyone in New York has problems,
hopefully yours will work out, excuse me (walks past her)

She see's that his heart has hardened and tries
another way. Danielle comes to hug

Nelson- (grabbing her arms) don't touch me
Danielle-look I'm sorry
Nelson- (Dark energy) don't touch

Nelson pulls away

Danielle-Please!
Nelson-move
Danielle-people are depending on you
Nelson-where's my keepers, my dependers?
Danielle- I'm here
Nelson-nobody with me
Danielle-I care
Nelson-NOBODY…well…somebody… its over, fuck her,fuck
you and your Jew history and hail Hitler for killing millions of
your people, and my only regret is he failed to kill your
grandparents so I wouldn't have to put up COCKING your slimy
jew pussy
Danielle- why you trying to be something you're not

220

Danielle tries to kiss him, but he pulls her hair screaming to the floor

Old man- girl are you ok?
Nelson- (pulls out an icepick) MINDYA FUCK'N BUSINESS
Old man- I'm gonna get the cops (looks at Danielle) don't worry missy, I'll be back
Danielle- NO! I mean (quietly) He's my boyfriend
Old man- you think you're tuff' beat'n on a woman!
Danielle- he didn't hit me I fell
Old man- yea right (looking furious) in my time you'd be shot in the face!
Nelson- (throws the pick over to the foot of the old man) how bout' stabbed in the face (walks over)
Danielle- NO! (trying to pull Nelson away)
Nelson- do it

Standoff is short lived

Old man- (kicks the pick under a parked car) one way trip to the big house kid (looks at Danielle walking off) find ya'self a decent guy, this bums goin nowhere
Danielle- please, I can take care of myself

The man leaves but looks back one last time muttering incoherently

Nelson goes to fetch the weapon
Danielle grabs him but he pushes her, she then runs to the car, reaching under, retrieving it first

Ice pick is now behind her back

Nelson- give it to me
Danielle-no

Nelson- (slaps her) GIVE IT TO ME

Danielle-(defiantly) NO!
Nelson- (closes his hand into a clenched fist) Danielle this is the last time, I'm not playing, GIVE ME THE KNIFE
Danielle-over my dead body
Nelson- GIVE IT TO ME!
Danielle- NO!

      Nelson Rears to strike, but as he comes forward, Danielle with her other hand brings forth the wooden Oscar

  Nelson- (Jerks his body, stopping momentum) who gave you that? (he stumbles backward)
Danielle- (she then brings forth the ice-cutter in the other hand) choose
Nelson-(weak) what?
Danielle- (carefully) *choose one…*

      Shot from uptop, reveals a strange image on the wall
      behind them disappear, finally she's pierced him
      Nelson has his back to the wall ready to fall.
      He seems lost, disorientated, frightened if you will of
      Danielle's presence. She see's his metal melting and
      moves at snails pace, reaching him eventually

  Danielle- (kisses him gently) can you hear that
Nelson- no, (teeth clattering) can't hear a thing

      An echo is heard through the wind

      "For Best lead performance by male, thee Academy
      goes too…"

Nelson- wait… (looks out his senses) I hear it, (shrieks) WHO'S THERE!
Danielle- it's your life
Nelson-*my life*
Danielle- yes, it's calling

Nelson- (falls to his knees and closes his eyes) so tired (voice eclipsing) tired girl

Danielle walks over creating footsteps in the snow, placing the wooden oscar in his shirt pocket, with her hair frosty white

Both are breathing smoke like poured steam, it's biting cold, with not person in sight

Nelson- (he holds her around the thighs) please don't leave
Danielle- (drops pick, then kneels) I'm right here (wraps her arms around him)
Nelson- alone
Danielle- you'll never be... alone

She continues to hold on, as more snow fall around them
@}-'-,-- -- **6**
View pans up over Lincoln Center and down streets of Ninth ave, soaring above the skyline of the city, topping off at the Empire State, where tinkles and scenery fade into a mist of silver clouds, storming over Manhattan

Slowly everything descends
Total darkness blinds the screen

~Till radio is heard fading in

Radio- Yowsers, and blue blazes, it seems the GroundHog missed his shadow this year and Spring is gonna be lil' young for it's britches, as we're seeing summer like weather this Easter nine one, more on the...

~"bad" from U2's wide awake in America begins to play

Flash 1- Shot of Grand Central Station, clock face on six o'clock

Flash 2- Lightbulbs lining a stretch of mirrors, where kids are checking their make up and changing attire. Farooz wears a Chaplin style hat helping Chantae with blush

Flash 3- Statue of Liberty, staring blankly into an ocean of stars glistening in the background

Flash 4- Raven and Bella hugging Danielle, apparently burying the hatchet with her (Raven and Bella are in spandex, pasted with twirls of psychedelic color)

Flash 5- Slow overview of Broadway all the way down the "Great White Way'" to Time Square

Flash 6- Abdul and Micheal polishing up routine, both dressed "Jackson Five"style, sporting fake Afro's

Flash 7- Glimpse of NBC studio's, starting at Atlas, then below the skating rink, panning up toward forty Rockefeller rooftop, better known as "Top of the Rock"

Flash 8- Audience filing in Oxford auditorium, as Joyce and Nadja the school guards are holding glow sticks, directing traffic. Joyce is having a dispute with Taheem and Lamott, as Hendrix and brother's floss in, brightly hued with yellow green shirts

Flash 9- Southstreet Seaport, lights of the ships and boathouses reflecting off the East river, to crescent moon in the sky, as the song "bad" comes to close

Flash 10- LaTanya passes Nelson giving him a pinch "Here comes Arsenio!" then hurry's off, as the producer comes through, Bridge

Nelson- Well we didn't get dressed up for nutt'n
Mr.Bridge- (smiling) we certainly didn't

Curtains open

The show begins

Booming voice- We're going to take you back! Way Back! Back into time!

Abdul with fake Chuck Berry hair do, holding an electric guitar, suddenly appears in a diner. He instantly introduces solo of "Johnny, be good"

Girls come out the sides with fifties style hairdo's and dresses, very colorful, going bonkers for Chuck

It's a short rendition of the song and after the first verse and chorus "Johnny be good" ends, being replaced by a ballad. "Magic changes" from the motion picture soundtrack "Grease"

Guys now show up on stage, Michael comes in first, looking like John Travolta, snapping out a switchcomb, combing his hair back very prima-donna, watching all the girls, which seem to be in two groups, one with lettered sweaters (W), and the others in long dress, begin to huddle and giggle, oogling at him.

Farooz and Danielle can be seen on rollerskates balancing trays with malts and sodapop, floating around stopping from place to place letting off goodies and napkins, or taking out pens, writing down orders

Abdul comes in next, along with another boy in the show who usually keeps to himself, his name is Ray and they meet up with Mike in the middle. Ray, Abdul, and Michael all look alike, with black leather MC jackets and slick backed hair
Three girls confront the gang of boys. LaTanya goes to Ray and leans on him, Kyoko goes to Abdul, and Bella who wasn't suppose to be in the sequence ends up with Michael

They dance slowly till the ballad ends

As the song dies out, Nelson comes in looking like "Buster Pointdexter" bi-focals and all

Ray taps Michael on the shoulder and whispers in his ear pointing at Nelson, suddenly Mike pulls off Bella and stomps toward Nelson, who is walking around trying to fit in

Bella can be seen pulling on Mike to leave him alone, but too late. Nelson turns after being turned down by a group of girls to dance and bumps right into Michael's chest, which he does not take kindly too. He gestures wildly to his boys to which they laugh exaggerated, then turns Nelson's front pocket inside out followed by a knocking off the glasses, which slide across the floor

Nelson runs to get his bi-focals, just missing a kick in the ass by Abdul

Bella storms off
Michael doesn't notice her absence, being too busy cackling with the fella's

Suddenly the song changes
"Hand Jive" blows in and both group of girls separated come together, doing the Dance.

Mike and company struggle with the Jive and show their frustration by isolating themselves in a corner, acting cooler then ever, but at this point none caring

Bella is seen doing the dance happily with the group of letter sweater girls she's with, until she's interrupted by LaTanya that her boyfriends back

Mike- LETS GO (grabs Bella)
Bella- get off'a me you JERK!

She yanks hard, but falls from the effort. Mike walks away

Nelson steps through being insulted by everything he passes and reaches down for her. She eyes him a moment, then takes his hand, being raised from the floor

Bella-thanks
Nelson- (walking away, head down) no problem
Bella-WAIT!

Nelson freezes to the spot

She glides over to him

Bella- dance with me

The whole stage watches

Nelson waits... Then turns the pocket Michael turned inside out back in and steps to Bella, where he takes off his glasses like Clark Kent, tossing them to the audience, to which they scream and…

Executes the "HandJive" and "LindyHop" better then Elvis himself

Not person who payed for ticket is left in thier seat. Audience is up and moving

Everybody on stage or down rows is dancing. Bella stops and gets closer to Nelson as if ready to kiss, but soon as she comes in for the kill, Danielle rolls by and taps him on the shoulder

Nelson lets go of Bella and turns to Danielle

Michael appears instantly behind Bella, fuming

Nelson- (to Danielle) hold on

He goes over to Mike's gang and centers himself between them

Nelson does the Jive to his left where Ray is standing showing him the move, then to his right where Mike is. When he repeats it to Ray they do it together, and when he turns to Mike, Mike busts it out right on cue

In unison they do a complicated form of the step, where three people slap and turn hands sequentially. The three take steps to the front, rhythmically tap dancing their hands across each other

As the song reaches its climax, members of the show break off in two lines, with girls on one side and boys on the other, beginning the chain reaction or Rock'n Roll ritual called "The Stroll" where other dances more difficult than "the Jive" (Lamda Nu, Jitterbug) can be showcased, as the end pair of the line come dancing down together reaching the front, the pair moves aside, as the next couple begins "Strolling". Chantell and Chantae are doing the "Charleston" LaTanya is doing the "Lindy Hop" with Ray, and Abdul is "Buffalo Strutting" with Kyoko

Michael whips out his switchcomb, snaps it open and combs his hair for the last time

Michael-HeyBuster! (snaps the comb closed and slaps it in Nelson's hand) lata'Daddy-0
Nelson-Thanks! (Watching Mike run to Bella lifting her off her feet, bringing her down kissing)

Strangely Nelson is alone again, same as when the
scene started, staring intently at the ground when out of
nowhere

Danielle- I told you, you'd make a great nerd

Nelson slides over to Danny and holds her
close, forgetting that there's an actual show on,
which he's the centerpiece of

Nelson- We *have* to work on our communication

Danielle smiles and they kiss passionately right on stage

The crowd goes wild

Danielle's father- (getting up) HEY! That's not in the script!
Danielle's mother- (pulling her husband) Neither is this (she
does the same as little Danielle and smootches her hubby)

Nelson and Danny are too busy to notice the
"Fifties" sequence of the show has ended. The curtains close
with them embraced in passion

AudienceEXPLODES into applause

Back behind the curtains lip'play is interrupted by
the producer

Mr.Bridge- eh,hmm (handing back his ill-advised, chucked
spectacles)
Nelson- (blushing) I'm sorry Mr. B, I know I was suppose to
do the split, (nervous) I'promise I'll make it up…

Bridge is not alone

Lady in White- do you know how hard it's been to get a hold
of you

Nelson stands mystified

Mr. Bridge- (grinning) I'll leave you two, to it (Mastering the Ceremonies, disappears)
Nelson- Do I know you?
Lady in White- no (she opens the curtains slightly) but your friends do ← *p.26

Nelson peaks out and see's Seph and Alec immediately jump to their feet like Banshees

Alec-YOU GOT THE PART 'YOSHI
Seph- (pointing right at him) I LOVE THIS KID!

She closes the cloth and reaches in her bag

Nelson- I'm sorry (suspensed) whats' going on?
Lady in White- let's just say (handing him a script) we have to talk

Nelson finally realizes what he's holding in his hand and begins to faint, but before knocking out

Lady in White- better hold that till later cutie (see's a girl run in from the changing area) looks like you still have a show to finish
LaTanya-(who's this strange woman-vibe) Nelson Motown's coming up
Mr.Bridge- NELSON!!!
Nelson- (turns blinking nervous) sorry
Mr. Bridge- ARE YOU CRAZY? YOU ONLY HAVE A

MINUTE TO CHANGE!
Nelson- uh, uhh (cut off)
Mr.Bridge-UH'NUTT'N! GET BACK THERE AND COSTUME UP! (Bridge winks to the Lady before heading back)

Nelson- sorry, but I have to go (runs frantically, taking off his belt to which his high waters drop, almost tripping himself turning the corner)

Lady in White smiles as Nelson turns the corner half naked

Danielle sitting under the bulbs watches him scutter back, holding something

Nelson- Gangway! Watch out (drops his posession in chair and heads off to the rack to get his Afro)
Danielle- (looks down, see's a script with a business card clipped on) what's this?
Nelson-(back with gray bellbottoms and pink long sleeve, butterfly collar) how much time! (hands crazy, fixing himself)
Danelle- (plucks card out) who's Lauren Ida Bergman
Nelson-(finally notices) oh some lady gave me that notices Chantae and Chantell standing stageleft, on mark and set) tink' it's starting
Danielle-it says "Broadway"
Nelson- Yeah I know (throws his glasses off and steps to the curtain) juicy ain't it (flings cloth aside, bolts out)

Danielle looks up from holding the card and gently blows a kiss to where Nelson just was, then picks up his nerd glasses from the prior performance and places them on her eyes, waiting a brilliant moment before whispering

"Wonderboy"

Scene retreats quietly, becoming smaller and smaller with Danielle sitting in her chair.

Outside Junior High "QuincyX.Oxford" Sal's pizzeria is closing up, amongst a slew of Eastside tree's embedded to a crystal skyline of the city. Far off in flight, spearheading the sky above Herald Square is the Empire State building, casting an illuminating blue above the heart of New York. And further off, can be seen the World Trade Center, ghostly waving ol'Glory on top it's Sterling feedom, which Americans once called…

"The Twin Towers"

@}-'-,------

www.ingramcontent.com/pod-product-compliance
Lightning Source LLC
Chambersburg PA
CBHW051456170626
46811CB00002B/514